READ BETWEEN THE LIES

Poppy Perkins Mystery #2

JASMINE WEBB

Chapter 1

THIS WAS ONE OF THE BEST DAYS OF MY LIFE. AND if you've been stabbed less than a week ago and you can still say that, it means life is on the upswing.

I was sitting inside One Market Restaurant, an upscale place across the street from the Ferry Building, popular with businesspeople on power lunches.

And that was exactly what I was doing now—having a power lunch with my new editor at Leon Books, the company that had just signed me onto their roster to write a book for them.

It still felt a bit like a dream. Like none of this was real.

FIVE DAYS EARLIER, I WAS LYING IN MY HOSPITAL bed. Twenty-four hours before that, I stopped a deranged murderer from killing my new friend

Ophelia and got a knife in the shoulder for my trouble. The doctors had told me I'd be discharged later that day after getting a visit from a physiotherapist who would run me through the first exercises I'd have to do to regain full mobility of my left arm. It was funny, in a way, that it took me being stabbed to get me to exercise.

Suddenly, Angie, my agent, appeared. She swung the privacy curtain aside with a flourish and entered my space, grinning from ear to ear.

"Babe, I have the best news ever! Your book is not only garnering interest, but you're in the best situation you could possibly hope for: a bidding war."

My mouth dropped open. "Seriously?"

"I wanted to tell you the good news in person. This way, we can celebrate."

Angie reached into the oversized jacket she'd been wearing and pulled out a full-sized bottle of Moet and Chandon, which she placed on the small table in front of my bed. Then, she reached into her purse and pulled out two glass champagne flutes.

I raised an eyebrow. "I'm not sure the nurse would appreciate seeing this."

"Live a little! You're in a bidding war. Just because it's a hospital doesn't mean it has to be depressing."

Angie opened the bottle of champagne. I winced at the popping sound of the cork, certain that someone was about to come in and tell us off.

"I'm not sure I should be drinking that with the drugs I'm on," I said, motioning to the IV sticking out of my arm.

"All the alcohol will do is make the morphine more fun. Come on. Just a little glass. You're going to be an author, babe!"

At those words, a warmth flowed through my veins, enveloping me in a hug. I was going to be an author. There was a bidding war over my book. No amount of champagne could give me the warm and fuzzies as much as those words did.

When Angie handed me a glass, I clinked it with hers and smiled. This was going to change my life.

I took a sip, letting the fuzzy bubbles sit on my tongue for a second before swallowing, and I laughed. "I can't believe it. An actual bidding war?"

"It's great. And now, we have to talk strategy. What are you looking for? Is there one company in particular you want to work with? Are you willing to go to New York often, or do you want to work with a smaller, local company?"

I looked Angie in the eye. "I'd love to work with Leon Books."

She barked out a laugh. "Petty little bitch, aren't you? I love it. Okay, I'm good friends with one of their acquiring editors; I'll get in her ear about this. I can't make any guarantees, but I'll do what I can."

I wanted to go with Leon Books because that was who Juliette, my former best friend, had signed with. After stealing one of my ideas and passing it off as her own.

"Yeah, I'd like to say I'm a bigger person than that, but I'm not. She stole from me, and I want to rub it in her face."

"Good for you. Spite is my favorite motivator. Now, how's your shoulder?"

"I'm alive, and it'll be fine, so I'm considering it a win."

"See if they'll give you some extra morphine to take home," Angie said with a wink. "I have to get going. I'll see what I can do for you with that deal, and I'll be in touch tonight or tomorrow."

She left with a flourish, like a tornado made of glitter, and if it wasn't for the champagne flue sitting at my side, I'd wonder if Angie had even been here at all.

Yesterday, I officially accepted an offer from Leon Books: eighty-two thousand dollars and right of first refusal for my next two books after this one.

I'd signed all the documents over Zoom, and now I was meeting my new editor. For the first time in my life, I was having a business lunch.

The hostess had led me to one of the two-person tables inside the restaurant, her kitten heels clicking along the stone tile. Long, bench seating on one side, and comfortable chairs on the other. I took the bench and ran my fingers along the hem of the tablecloth as I sat down. This place was fancy.

"Thanks," I said as the woman handed me a

menu, but the butterflies in my stomach weren't hungry. This was the biggest meeting of my life. I slipped my phone from my purse to check the time; it was three minutes to twelve.

About a minute later, my new editor slipped into the chair across from me.

Ellie Jacobs was about five foot three, with black hair in tight waves that reached down to her shoulders. Her cat's-eye glasses had thick, deep mauve frames, and her lipstick matched them exactly. Dressed in a cute blouse and black pants, with a Michael Kors bag at her side, Ellie looked like the perfect mid-twenties-something professional.

"Poppy," she greeted me, her voice warm and soft. "It's so nice to meet you. I'm Ellie."

"It's really nice to meet you too."

Ellie sat down and leaned across the table. "This is your first contract, right? Exciting!"

"It is. I'll admit; I've been dreaming of this day for a long time."

"Well, I'll tell you what I tell all my aspiring authors: this industry is one of the hardest in the world to break into. But if you manage it, you'll achieve things most people could never dream of."

"I'm not one to scare off easy," I said with a wry smile.

Ellie gaze fell to my injured shoulder. "No, you don't look it. I wanted to meet with you today so the two of us could get to know each other. I've seen your brief and read the first few chapters of your book. They're great. The foundation is there, and I'm sure together we're going to create something incredible. I don't usually sign books on spec, but in your case, I wanted to make an exception because I love the concept so much, and the chapters you've written show that you'll be able to do that story justice. So, tell me, why Leon Books?"

I smiled warmly at Ellie. No way was I going to tell her the full truth, but this was a version of it. "I like that Leon has an arm in San Francisco, so I don't have to travel to New York constantly just to meet with my editor. I like the books you've got published, I think you're on the cutting edge of the industry right now, and I want to hitch my wagon to you long-term."

"That's so great to hear. And I love that we're in the same city. It's going to be easier to connect, although, full disclosure—most of our discussions will be online. It's just easier that way."

"Totally understood."

"Great. Do you have any questions for me?"

For the next half hour or so, Ellie and I discussed exactly what my new project was going to entail as we ate a phenomenal lunch. I ordered the trout so that I could still cut it even with one of my arms in a full sling. By the time we finished eating, I had a better idea of exactly how our working relationship would unfold.

"So, have you lived here your whole life?" I asked Ellie, and she shook her head.

"No. I grew up on the East Coast and came here for college. I went to Stanford, majored in math. I ended up realizing my choices were to stay in academia for the rest of my life, or go into tech. Neither one of them really attracted me, and I switched to English. I've always loved reading, and while studying, I realized this was what I wanted to do with my life. I wanted to take books and help make them better. I'm not good at writing stories from scratch, but it turns out I can take something that exists, and I love to try to improve it."

"You really are in the right job, then."

"Exactly. Leon Books took me on as an intern in my second year, straight-up hired me in my third and fourth years, and gave me an offer right off the bat after I graduated. I've been with them my whole working life."

"That's really cool. And you like it there?"

"I do. All my coworkers are fantastic. And it's a challenging job. The last thing I wanted was to end up in a position where I spent every day just going through the motions, turning off my brain and waiting for the clock to hit five o'clock. But here, I don't have that at all. My days are busy. I'm either going through books, working with cover designers, speaking with representatives from the bookstores… It's great. I'm not going to lie."

"Sweet. I know exactly what you mean. I didn't mind working at San Techcisco Donuts, but it was a retail job. I was good at it, but it didn't mentally stimulate me very much. It was all about giving people what they wanted, selling up, that sort of thing."

Ellie's eyes fell to my sling. "I heard about what happened. I didn't want to bring it up; it felt rude."

"Oh, don't worry about it. The entire internet has seen the video that led to this happening," I said with a smile, pulling my sling forward a bit and holding it up. "I'm fine with talking about it."

"What are you going to do now? Work-wise, I mean?"

"I'm not sure," I admitted. "It's only been a few days since I've been released from hospital, and this book deal has taken up most of my mental energy."

"Understandable."

"I guess I'll just have to go out and find another job. The doctor said in two weeks I can get rid of the sling, so that should make things easier, since right now no one will want to hire a retail worker who's only got one functional arm."

"I dunno. I hear a lot of places are pretty desperate for staff these days," Ellie said with a grin. "It's smart that you're going to keep another job while working on your book too. I know the overall money is a good deal, but you're not going to see all of it straight away."

The contract Leon Books had sent over and which I'd signed laid everything out for me. The advance was for eighty-two thousand dollars. I'd received twelve thousand on signing—my bank account breathed an *enormous* sigh of relief when it was deposited—and the rest would come in chunks. Twenty thousand when I reached the deadline to have half the book finished. Another twenty when the book was complete. Fifteen thousand more after edits. And the final fifteen thousand when the book was published. That date was scheduled to be a year from now.

"Exactly. Besides, while it's not the most mentally stimulating work, being in retail gives me the chance to people-watch in a way an office job wouldn't let me."

Ellie chuckled. "I bet."

She paid the bill, and the two of us headed out into the street.

"Come on, let's go back to the office together. I'll introduce you to some of the people who will help make this series sell," Ellie suggested.

"That sounds great." The Leon Books offices were a few blocks west of here, and we began walking together, chatting comfortably. It felt like I'd known her for years, rather than just for an hour.

To our left, one of the cable cars, loaded with tourists, clanged its bell, announcing it was about to stop. We joined the throngs of people just finishing up their lunches and walking back to the office on the extra-wide red-brick sidewalk.

"Do you need any help with anything?" Ellie asked. "You know, what with your arm?"

"Thanks, but I'm fine. I have a couple of friends

who own the coffee shop under me. They're making sure I've got enough groceries."

"Good. It's nice to have friends in this city."

"It is. San Francisco is a nice place for that."

Ellie nodded. "It's a much friendlier place than New York. I mean, sure, it's still a big city, but this is a place where people will still smile at you on the street and you can strike up a conversation with a stranger next to you."

Suddenly, we reached a large crowd and were jostled just slightly. At one point, Ellie stumbled back away from me. I turned and looked at her— and gasped.

She was clutching at her abdomen, blood pouring through her fingers, a red patch expanding outward from her shirt.

She looked up at me, her eyes wide, mouth open.

And then Ellie collapsed face-first onto the pavement.

Chapter 2

I IMMEDIATELY RUSHED TO HER SIDE, ROLLING Ellie over with my free hand.

"Someone call 911," I shouted. A couple of passersby had stopped to help.

"I'm a nurse," someone said, pushing me aside. I let her take over, and I stood up, scanning the street. Someone had obviously just stabbed Ellie. But who?

About a hundred feet away, one person was walking faster than the rest. I didn't think; I took off after them. That nurse was going to take better care of Ellie than I could, anyway.

The person walking away wore a dark green hoodie with the hood up. As I started running, they looked behind and must have spotted me. I couldn't make out their facial features. They were too far away. Somewhere between five six and five eleven?

The hoodie and baggy sweats made it impossible to make out their weight, or even gender.

As soon as they saw me, the person turned and bolted. I gave chase, but it was hard. I had never been a runner. Here in San Francisco, I rode my bike everywhere, so it wasn't like I was the least fit person on the planet. I just hated running. As a result, I wasn't good at it.

It also didn't help that one of my arms was strapped into a sling pressed against my chest, giving me even less power than I normally would have had.

Still, whoever this was, they'd just stabbed Ellie. I was sure of that. I wasn't going to let them get away if I could help it. Letting the adrenaline coursing through my body propel me forward, I sprinted toward Ellie's attacker.

I started gaining ground; the mass of people at the busy lunch hour stopped the attacker from full-on sprinting to get away. I was getting closer. My lungs burned, and my vision was starting to blur around the edges, but I was going to get them. Suddenly, however, when I was about ten feet away from them, the attacker darted into the street and directly in front of one of the cable cars.

I gasped, stopping in my tracks to avoid getting hit by the cable car. Had the attacker been hit? No. The cable car didn't stop. I waited for it to pass, and when it did, I darted out into the street, and that's when I realized the attacker had jumped on.

Their forest-green hoodie faced away from me as the cable car trundled along.

I shouted in vain at the conductor to stop, but it was too noisy and moving too fast, and I knew even as I was calling out to him that there was no way he could possibly hear me.

A car behind me honked, and I realized I was standing in the middle of the street.

I waved an apology as I stepped back onto the sidewalk then rushed back to where I'd left Ellie.

A crowd had gathered around her now, and I pushed through it until I reached the front. The sight that met me made my throat dry up.

She was lying, eyes closed, on the pavement. The contents of her purse had spilled onto the sidewalk next to her: an open notepad with some math stuff scribbled on it, her phone in a *Star Wars* case, a Michael Kors wallet, a couple of tampons. Someone had wrapped up a jacket and placed it under her head as a pillow. The nurse was sitting back on her haunches, looking sadly down at Ellie. She hadn't made it. She was dead.

"Ellie," I whispered, dropping down next to her.

"The ambulance is here," someone called out. "Make room for the EMTs."

But they were too late.

My head swam with thoughts as the EMTs

arrived and confirmed what we already knew. Who would have done this to Ellie? Was it a random attack? One of those things you hear about on the news and never assume will happen to you? Or had someone in her life followed her and done this to her?

I knew who I had to call.

My hand trembled slightly as I pulled out my phone and dialed Ophelia's number.

"Poppy," she answered warmly on the second ring. "How are you doing?"

"I'm fine, but there's a body at my feet belonging to my new editor, who's just been murdered."

Ophelia's tone immediately went serious. "Where are you?"

"The corner of Market and Drumm."

"Don't move. I'll be there in five minutes."

Ophelia ended the call, and I sat next to Ellie. All around me, people were moving. Talking. One of the EMTs was on the phone, probably to the police. Another was trying to keep the crowd away from Ellie's body. A third crouched next to me and asked me if I was all right. I nodded, but I barely noticed him talking to me at all. The people around me were all like shadows in my periphery. I couldn't get my eyes off Ellie. She was younger than me, maybe twenty-five, twenty-six. And now she lay here, dead. Who could have done this to her?

"Poppy," a voice next to me said. I stood and

found myself looking at Ophelia. Tall, with a stature that made her seem larger than life, Ophelia wore an open camel-colored trench coat over a black turtleneck and skinny jeans, with a white Prada purse on her arm, as always. Her eyes were full of concern. "How are you holding up?"

"Uh, fine, I think. It's just... She was my editor. She was nice. I don't know what happened. Sorry, I don't know why I called."

"Because of all your friends, I'm the only one who hunts murderers for a living?" Ophelia offered with a sympathetic smile.

I let out a burst of nervous laughter. "Yeah. That's it. I know the governor hasn't called you in on this one, and it's probably not the sort of thing you normally do..."

"One of the great things about being me is that I get to do whatever I want," Ophelia replied, shooting me a wink. "So, start by telling me: what happened here?"

"I don't know. We were just walking along. We'd just finished having lunch. She was taking me back to the office so I could meet some people. It was busy, there were people around, and then all of a sudden, she wasn't with me anymore. I stopped to look, and she was clutching her stomach, blood pouring out of it. She collapsed. That woman there said she was a nurse and pushed me out of the way to take care of her. I got up and looked to see who had done it. I'm pretty sure I spotted them. Hoodie

15

and sweatpants. They saw me and ran. I gave chase, and I almost caught them, but they hopped onto a cable car and got away. By the time I got back here, Ellie was dead."

Ophelia nodded as she looked at the body, her eyes moving to the items on the ground. "Do you know of anyone who would want Ellie dead?"

"No. She didn't mention anything that would have given me the slightest indication. Not a thing. I mean, we mostly talked business too. It's not like we were best friends. I met her for the first time today."

"Okay. All the same, consider me on the case. The police will be here soon; you know the drill."

"Don't talk to them."

"Exactly. I'll organize a chat at the station again when Sameen arrives. Are you going to be a suspect here?"

"I'm not sure. I don't think I should be. But you never know."

Ophelia looked around. "Ideally, there should be security footage from around here. I'd like to have any available video of the murder. I assume the killer took the murder weapon with them?"

I nodded. "Yes. She was just bleeding. I'm assuming she was stabbed."

"Looks likely," Ophelia said. She reached into her purse and pulled out a pair of latex gloves, which she pulled on before kneeling next to Ellie and carefully pulling back the hem of her shirt.

Read Between the Lies

"Hey," one of the EMTs called out. "Don't touch the body until the police get here."

"It is fine; I work with the police," Ophelia replied. "They should be arriving shortly, anyway. Look at that, Poppy. That wound. It was most certainly made by a blade, and a sharp one. Single-edged and about an inch wide. She was stabbed. There is no question about it."

"So the killer did take the knife with them," I said thoughtfully.

"Yes, a risky strategy, to avoid having it traced back to them."

Sirens in the distance grew louder, and Ophelia put the shirt back into place and removed her gloves as we waited for the police to arrive. She took another look at the notebook then pulled out her phone and took a photo of what was written on it. As soon as the police cars pulled up, the crowd moved back. Four police officers emerged from squad cars and immediately set about securing the scene with yellow police tape, pushing back the onlookers.

Beyond them, a man I recognized stepped forward, dressed in slacks and a dark blue shirt, a scowl on his face. It was Detective Morello, the man who thought I'd killed tech billionaire Jason Bergman only a couple of weeks ago.

"You again," he snarled, and I was genuinely unsure if he meant that comment for me, or for Ophelia.

Ophelia rose to her full stature. "It's lovely to see you again, too, Detective Morello."

"What are you doing here this time, Ophelia?"

"I solve murders. One of us has to do it."

"I'm the one who arrests people."

"You're right. And on that note, I'd like my silver platter back, when you get a chance," Ophelia replied.

Having no comeback to that, Detective Morello turned to me. "And you. What are you doing at another one of my murder scenes?"

"Sorry, not without my lawyer," I replied with a self-satisfied smile. Detective Morello had tried to nail me for murder once. I wasn't about to give him a second shot at it.

"Fine. Meet me at the station in two hours. I'll need a statement from you, then, since I'm obviously not getting one now."

Ophelia gently led me away from the crime scene. It wasn't until we were a couple of blocks away that I realized I was trembling.

"Are you all right?" she asked.

"I… I think so. I guess it's weird. This is the second murder I've seen in two weeks."

"Sometimes, life likes to drop all the lemons in your lap at once."

"No kidding. At least Jason Bergman was kind of a dick. Ellie was nice. I mean, I barely knew her, but I liked her. She took a chance on me, someone she didn't know. That was good of her. And now I don't know what's going to happen with my book. I guess it'll get handed to another editor."

"Yes, I would imagine so."

"Thanks for coming. Is Sameen available? I guess I'll talk to the police and then leave them with the rest of the case."

Ophelia smiled as we walked along, the direction we were taking letting me know that we were headed for her office. "Oh, I don't know. There are a couple of things about this case that I find very interesting, and I have some spare time right now. What do you say? Should we solve another murder together?"

I raised my eyebrows. "Sure, yeah. If you're interested. I'd love to join you. Although I'd prefer it if this time doesn't end with me getting stabbed."

"I can't make that promise, but I'll do my best to prevent it from happening this time. How is your arm?"

"It's a little sore, but I'll survive," I said, rolling my shoulder gingerly in the socket and wincing from the pain. As it turns out, running after a murderer isn't the best thing for your arm, even if it's in a sling.

"I have ice in the fridge at the office. And you'll need some new clothes too."

I looked down to see my outfit was splattered with blood. It must have transferred onto me when I rolled Ellie over.

"I don't think we're the same size," I said wryly.

"Luckily for you, you wouldn't be the first one of my clients who needed a change of wardrobe at my office."

"I assume you don't have Girl Scouts in England? Because if they did, you would have crushed everyone else in your troop. I've never met anybody as prepared as you are."

Ophelia laughed good-naturedly. "Thank you."

We reached Ophelia's office building in SoMa, the trendy business district of San Francisco. The red-brick building with a green façade made me think of the gold rush era, and when we entered, we took the elevator to the discreet third floor that housed Ophelia's office.

The elevator doors opened onto the office with its dark wooden walls and light grey tile. Skylights in the ceiling lit the space, and track lighting added a warm glow. At the end of the hall was the main conference room, and that's where Ophelia and I ended up. She placed her bag on the enormous wooden table while I sank into one of the dozen Eames chairs surrounding it.

"It's the math, isn't it?"

"Isn't what?"

"What's interesting you in this case. She had a bunch of math in that notebook."

Ophelia smiled. "You are observant. Yes. She was an editor for a publishing company. And yet, she had a notebook with some extremely advanced maths."

"She told me she studied math in college but decided it wasn't for her, so she switched to English and went into publishing."

"Did she really? That is interesting in and of itself."

"Do you recognize it? The math, I mean."

Ophelia shook her head. "No. Maths is not my strong suit; I have to admit. I can get by, but this is beyond my skill set. However, I have a friend that will be able to help. I've sent him a text, and he'll be here shortly. We will see what this is all about. And then we will decide how to proceed from there. Will this case be interesting? I suspect it will. Now, come with me. We will get you out of those bloody clothes."

Ten minutes later, I emerged from the bathroom wearing a new, crew-necked navy-blue sweatshirt with FBI written in yellow lettering in the top left corner. I did not want to know where Ophelia had gotten these, or even if they were official. I had a sneaking suspicion that they were.

I returned to the conference room to find another man who had also just entered. He was short, probably five foot five at the most, and a little bit on the chubbier side, dressed in Birkenstocks, shorts, and a grey T-shirt with a green flannel shirt open over it.

"Ah, Poppy. This is my friend Anthony Dwyer. He's a maths professor at Stanford, and he happened to be in the city right now. He's going to look at the work Ellie had on her notebook for us."

"It's nice to meet you," I said with a smile as I shook Anthony's hand. He didn't meet my eyes, and his handshake was very limp. But he nodded quickly.

"Yes. You as well. Now, what do you have?"

Ophelia tapped a couple of keys on her phone, and a moment later, the far wall was illuminated with a large version of the photo of Ellie's notebook. "This is what she had written down. Do you recognize it?"

Anthony and I looked at the screen. In the top corner of the page was a symbol. It looked almost like Ellie had drawn a tulip with a single pen stroke, but the left side was open.

Anthony frowned. "Yes. Or at least, I recognize what she's trying to solve here. She's using the Goldbach Conjecture. The layperson's explanation is that any even number over two can be expressed as the sum of two primes. She's got several figures here and is using the Goldbach Conjecture to split them into two other prime numbers that add up to her original figures."

"What numbers does she have?" Ophelia asked.

"The first solution was a split. She got 8,041,663 and 37 from 8,041,700. That one she's figured out herself. Then there are four other sets of numbers here. 449, 97, 433, 3, 19, 103, 509, and 5. But there's no solution here."

"They're coordinates," Ophelia said immediately. "San Francisco is at 37.8 degrees north. I suspect the other numbers will give us the latitude, if we add them up properly. Let's start off this way: which ones in that second set add up to 122?"

"103 and 19," Anthony replied immediately.

"Okay, so remove those. Everywhere in the San Francisco area is in that degree west, so it's safe to assume our coordinate is too. And the first figure went to seven digits in the decimal, so let's assume this one will as well."

"That narrows things down slightly; with the figures you've got, the 5 and 3 must combine to make an 8. Otherwise, every other figure will have too many digits. From there, the fastest way to do this if you can't narrow it down further will be trial and error," Anthony said. "Can I borrow a pen and paper?"

The man worked fast, scribbling figures down on the sheet, doing the math in his head. As he wrote down the numbers, I plugged them into Google Maps on my phone.

"That one puts us a few miles east of the Golden Gate," I said when I'd entered the first number. Anthony crossed it out.

"Then we need a smaller number, to bring it farther west," Anthony muttered, jotting down a second possibility.

"That one's right in the middle of Crissy Field," I said. "At least it's on land, though I'm not entirely sure why Ellie would have coordinates to a random part of the marsh."

Crissy Field used to be an army airfield but had now been restored into a large park and a public beach. The field had a boardwalk between the grass and the beach that offered one of the city's best views of the Golden Gate Bridge. Popular among locals, tourists, and the city's birders—you were practically guaranteed to see a heron if you looked long enough—it was one of the many green spaces in the city that made me truly fall in love with San Francisco.

"Okay, we have one other possibility nearby, then," Anthony said, scribbling down a third number.

I punched it into my app. "This one is on the other side of the bridge, in the Presidio. Right along the coastal trail, near the old batteries."

"I think that's more likely," Ophelia said slowly.

"What are you thinking? Why was Ellie trying to solve for coordinates?"

"Math competition," Ophelia and Anthony answered in unison.

"A math competition? Isn't that the sort of thing you do inside, in a school?"

"In an academic setting, yes," Anthony said, nodding vigorously. "But these days, things have changed. Math has become more hands-on. It affects our everyday lives in ways people even fifty years ago could never have imagined, and as a

Read Between the Lies

result, the way mathematicians interact and get attention has changed."

"So this competition, it's a real thing? How does it work?"

"They're generally run by corporations trying to recruit the best and brightest minds," Anthony said, speaking quickly, his eyes on the paper. "Sometimes they're cybersecurity companies, but as of recently, the bigger business is hedge funds. Crypto. Finance. The point is to find someone who can not only do the math but solve the riddles behind it. And these big corporations are the ones who can put up the prize for these competitions."

"What kind of prize are we talking about?" I asked.

"Generally, one to two million dollars."

My mouth dropped open. "You're joking. Are you serious?"

"To a hedge fund, that's practically petty cash. Finding the next big analyst who can write an algorithm to spot opportunities in the market can be worth hundreds of millions to these companies. Maybe even more."

"Well, I think we've got a pretty good motive for murder," I said, looking at Ophelia.

"Indeed," she said. "This is turning out to be quite interesting. Shall we go and visit the Presidio and see if we can't find the next clue?"

Chapter 3

OPHELIA THANKED ANTHONY, WHO LEFT SOON after, and she and I hopped into her sleek Audi sedan and sped off toward the other end of town.

"It's wild to me that this is a thing that exists. Math contests, like a nerdy adult version of a scavenger hunt but with a seven-figure prize and a job offer at the end of it. I know I've only lived here a year, but this city literally never stops surprising me. I had no idea this existed. What do you think we're going to find?"

"Frankly, I haven't got a clue. But I'm intrigued. And let's be honest; there's no way the police are going to figure out this motive the way we already have. Even if they do, they aren't going to get anywhere with it. Yes, this is already turning out to be an interesting case, and I think we should see it through."

"Let's do it. I haven't been stabbed in almost a week."

Ophelia laughed. "I'm glad you're handling it with a sense of humor."

"It would be depressing if I didn't."

"Have you told your mom yet? About the deal, I mean?"

"No. Technically, I also haven't told her about getting stabbed. I don't want the lecture that I know will be on its way if I do. I was waiting to tell her."

"Waiting for what? You signed the papers, didn't you?"

"I did, yeah. But there's still this little part of me that kind of thinks everything is going to go wrong. It doesn't make any sense, I know that. But it's the little bit of me that's doing it as self-preservation. If I don't allow myself to fully lean into what's happening, if bad things happen, then I won't feel as disappointed. And after facing so much disappointment when it comes to my publishing career—if you can even call it that—I guess I'm just trying to protect myself. Because the worst thing that could possibly happen would be telling my mom I have a book deal and then having it all fall apart because of something outside of my control. Like my editor getting murdered."

"While unfortunate, Ellie's death won't impact the contract that you signed. Regardless, you've got that deal. You just need to wait for Leon Books to assign you a new editor now."

"I know. As I said, it doesn't make any sense. But it's how I protect myself."

"You see it as protection, but that's really just fear with another name. What would happen if you let go of that fear and told your mother that you signed a contract for a book?"

A small smile crept up one corner of my mouth. "I'd get to tell her she was wrong about me. That I can be an author and that it was the right move to refuse to go to law school."

"You see? You're already happy thinking about it."

"But what if something goes wrong, and I have to go back and tell her that?"

"What if things go right?" Ophelia countered as she pulled into the parking lot near the Golden Gate overlook. Gravel crunched beneath the car tires as she parked the car beneath the small grove of trees that made up the center of the looping lot. The Presidio was one of the most incredible parks in America. Over 1,500 acres that had originally belonged to the Ohlone people. In 1776, the Spanish arrived and built a military fortification on the point, making it the first part of modern San Francisco to be settled by Europeans. In 1820, it passed to Mexico and in 1848, the United States, who used it as a military base until 1948, when it was passed on to the National Parks Service.

Today, it was a huge park, the perfect place to spend a gorgeous afternoon. Personally, I loved taking my bike and going for a casual ride, or hiking the over 20 miles of trails, which were where Ophelia and I were about to go. The lot where we parked linked up with the Batteries to Bluffs, one of the best easy hiking trails in the area. Located high on the bluffs, this trail connected, via a series of very long and steep staircases, some of the best beaches in town. The narrow, dusty single track offered some of the most incredible views over San Francisco and was dotted with old military batteries, concrete installations whose artillery had long since been removed. This was where we were headed now.

I checked my phone and the coordinates given. The location that corresponded to Ellie's figures were located not far from the parking lot. We went down to the trail, and I quickly realized where we were being taken.

"This battery," I said, motioning in front of us. "It's something here."

The concrete building had obviously seen better days. The grasses, shrubs, and weeds that surrounded it were starting to slowly take over the battery, growing over one of the upper walls. The concrete was dotted with metal doors, and the whole thing was covered in graffiti. Stairs led up to the upper levels, where the guns had once been held.

"Do you know what we're looking for?" I asked Ophelia.

She shook her head. "No. It's obviously a clue to

the next part of the math challenge. Let's split up and see what we can find."

"I guess we're looking for something that looks math-like and probably isn't that message there," I said, pointing at a wall where someone had painted "ILickBallz69" in yellow spray paint.

Ophelia snorted. "I'm going to assume you're right."

The two of us split up, with Ophelia taking the left side of the battery and me the right. I studied all the spray-painted symbols, messages, and paintings carefully, looking for something—anything—that could be a hint as to the next clue in the competition Ellie had been competing in.

About five minutes in, I had climbed the stairs to the top level, stepping over a large patch of weeds that had grown through the cracks in the concrete on one of the steps. I was glad we were here in October and not July; the sun beat down upon me, and the strong winds whipped at my hair. Still, I suddenly spotted something.

"Ophelia! Up here!"

Twenty seconds later, Ophelia bounded up the steps toward me. In the middle of this part of the battery was a raised, round platform, also made of concrete, where the large artillery guns would have been kept. On the wall in front of it was spray-painted that same tulip picture that I'd seen in the corner of Ellie's paper.

"That. She had it written down on her paper."

Ophelia nodded. "It's the Greek letter *phi*, in lowercase."

"Right," I said, trying to sound like I knew that all along and hadn't just been describing it as a tulip in my head. "It's got to be linked to the competition. That's too random a thing for someone to just graffiti here separately."

"I agree," Ophelia said, her eyes scanning the area around it. "Here. There are some more figures, painted in the same color as the *phi*. Let's get some pictures. Maybe Anthony can help us uncover what they're all about."

"What's the next step?" I asked. "After all, we could try and get Anthony to help us solve this, but how does that help us find Ellie's killer?"

"Yes, although it's early enough in the investigation that I'm keeping all avenues open. I'll have Anothny try to solve as much of this as he can, but I also think we should stay here and stake out this clue. See who arrives. After all, anybody else competing in this game is a suspect, for very obvious reasons."

"Hey," someone suddenly called out from behind us. "You. What are you doing here?"

I turned to find myself staring at a woman holding out a can of pepper spray at us. My eyes immediately widened, which, in retrospect, probably wasn't the best way to go. I took a step back, but Ophelia just smiled.

"You're competing in the maths competition,

aren't you?" she asked the woman. Around five foot six, in her twenties, with ink-black eyes and matching hair that hung down to her shoulders, she was dressed casually in jeans and a black T-shirt.

"Yeah. And so are you."

"No. We're investigating the murder of one of your fellow competitors."

The woman narrowed her eyes. "Bull. You're just telling me that to scare me off. It's not going to work. This clue is mine. And I can make sure you're delayed in going further."

"Under California law, you're only allowed to use that in self-defense," I said, motioning to the cannister in her hand with my chin.

"I'll say you attacked me."

"There's no need for that," Ophelia said. "We're telling the truth. We're not competing in this game; we're trying to find out who killed Ellie Jacobs."

"Wait, Ellie Jacobs was *here*? She was competing in this?"

I nodded. "Yes. And we're telling the truth about her death. Look at me. Do you remember when Jason Bergman was killed, and that video of the fight he had with a donut store employee just before he died was all over the internet? That was me."

The woman turned and looked at me carefully. I tried not to look at the pepper spray which she still had pointed directly at me. "It is you. Yeah."

"I'm not a math person. I'm a former donut

33

store employee and author. I was having lunch with Ellie when someone stabbed her, and she died. She had these coordinates on a piece of paper with her, and we're trying to find out who could have killed her."

"Ellie's really dead?" the woman asked, lowering the pepper spray.

"I'm sorry, yes," Ophelia replied softly. "You knew her, then?"

"Only by reputation. Ellie's a couple years older than me. She was a prodigy. One of the best mathematical minds in the country. She won the Putnam, the most prestigious math competition for undergrads. Until she quit, suddenly. No one knows why. She transferred to English, and I never heard about her again. Until now. She was actually in this competition? Damn."

I had a feeling this woman was telling the truth.

"Do you know anyone else involved in this competition?" Ophelia asked. "What's your name, by the way?"

"Mia. Mia Park. No, I don't know who else is involved. This is all very secret. But it's high-level stuff. I'm guessing there are only fifteen or twenty people in total."

"How did you find out about it?"

"There was a coded message posted in a group for math geeks. Only people who could spot the code and solve it would have been able to enter;

that's how they weed out the people who don't have a chance."

"When was this?" Ophelia asked.

"A week ago. The competition begins as soon as the message is posted. It took me a day to realize."

"What number clue is this?" I asked.

"Four."

"Do you know how many there are in total?"

"No. I just keep solving until I get to the end. And I hope I'm first. Or close enough to it that I'll get a good job offer all the same."

"You're working for Apple right now," Ophelia said.

Mia looked a little bit taken aback. "How do you know that?"

Ophelia motioned to the Converse on Mia's feet. "You've got the leaf of a persimmon tree caught in the lace of your shoes. They're far from the most common tree in these parts, but there are a number of them at Apple Park."

Mia swore as she reached down and grabbed the leaf, tossing it aside. "Fine. Yes, I work for Apple now. I'm an analyst there, but I'd love a Wall Street job. I want the million bucks. But I also want the job offer that goes with it."

"Do you know anyone else in the math world who might still be in touch with Ellie?" Ophelia asked.

"Look, you could try Oliver Dorchester."

Ophelia looked surprised. "The chess Grandmaster?"

"Yes. He lives in town now, and I know he and Ellie went to college together. If she kept in touch with anyone from that time, it probably would have been him."

"Can you send me the document you got that introduced the competition?" Ophelia asked.

"Sure. I'll AirDrop it to you," Mia said, pulling out her phone. "Someone really killed Ellie?"

"Yes. I don't say this to scare you, but although we don't know the reason at the moment, a million dollars is a very good motive. Please, be careful," Ophelia warned.

Mia shuddered. "Who kills people over *math*?"

That was what we were hoping to find out.

Chapter 4

After speaking with Mia for a few more minutes, we left her with the next clue on the wall of the battery and headed back to the car.

"Oliver Dorchester," I said. "I think even I've heard that name. He's the world champion, isn't he?"

"Yes, and very much considered the bad boy of the chess world."

I snorted. "There's a sentence that's never been uttered before."

"There are a lot of people who take the game very seriously. Oliver is currently ranked number three in the world. It's interesting that he knew Ellie."

"There's a lot of this that's interesting. I knew she studied math, but I had no idea she used to be a math prodigy. And yet she quit, officially, but she's still doing these competitions. It's weird."

"Perhaps. Ellie obviously enjoyed maths. We don't have to make a career out of something to still enjoy it. I think, in fact, if people took more time to learn things they were interested in, without the underlying pressure that society puts on us to turn everything we do into a money-making exercise, there would be a lot of happier people in the world."

"That's true. Maybe you're right. Maybe Ellie just decided she liked doing math for herself and not for anyone else. We'll find out, I guess."

"Yes. I also received a message from Sameen; she's going to join us at the police station so that you can give your statement. She also would like you to know that the police have found video footage of the crime, which clears you from suspicion."

"That's a relief, at least. Being the prime suspect in a crime wasn't the best time of my life."

"No. So you really are just going to give a statement and tell the police anything you can that might help."

I shrugged. "I'm not sure what I know. The killer had on a dark green hoodie, but if they have video footage, they'll already know that."

"Then that's what you tell them. They will do with that information as they will. As I've said before, if this case turns out to be linked to the math competition, I believe that Detective Morello will be found to be well outside of his depths. But they will run their investigation. We will run ours."

"Thank you," I said, turning to her. "I know you don't have to do this, but I appreciate that you are. I liked Ellie. We hit it off really well. She deserves justice."

"Indeed. I will see if I can find an address for Oliver Dorchester while you speak with Detective Morello."

This was my second time in the central San Francisco police station, and it was far less nerve-racking this time around. Instead of being taken to the interrogation room, with its one-way mirror, depressing grey paint, and off-kilter chair, I was led to Detective Morello's desk. Not that this location was much more comfortable, mind. The fluorescent light above flickered on and off, and the walls were a slightly less depressing beige that made you wonder if they were painted that color on purpose or originally supposed to be white. Oh, and the plain metal chair I'd been given wobbled.

If my lawyer, Sameen, noticed any of this, she didn't show it. She arrived about thirty seconds after I did and happily sat down in the chair next to me, offering me a smile.

"How are you holding up? This should be much easier than the last time around, but as always, if you aren't comfortable with anything, don't be afraid to refuse to answer."

"Have you seen the video footage they claim to have?" I asked.

"Yes. Wouldn't have let you answer these questions without it. There's no doubt about it: the killer knocked into Ellie and stabbed her then continued on as if it was an accident."

I shuddered. "Poor her. It's so awful."

Before Sameen had a chance to respond, Detective Morello arrived, plonking himself into his office chair, which wheezed in protest as it sank a couple of inches under his weight.

"All right, Ms. Perkins. I need a statement from you. We already know you didn't do this, so this time around, I'm just looking for anything you can tell me that will help."

"I wish I could, but I don't have much. Ellie and I had lunch together."

"How do you know her?"

"She's my editor. She was my editor. She worked for Leon Books, who I'd just signed a book deal with."

"Already? Wow, you might not have killed Jason Bergman, but you're certainly taking advantage of his death."

"My book has nothing to do with that, and I was already in the process of finding a publisher before he was killed. Besides, I'm not sure you're one to talk, given as you took credit for the arrest after Ophelia gave you all the evidence you needed on a silver platter."

Detective Morello scowled. "I would have figured it out eventually."

"Let's not say things we both know aren't true."

"Moving on," Detective Morello said between gritted teeth. "The two of you had lunch together. I assume it was scheduled?"

"Yes, we organized it yesterday afternoon. Ellie sent me the time and place."

"What happened when you left?"

"Ellie asked if I had some more time; she wanted to introduce me to a few other people at the office."

"Is that normal?"

I shrugged. "Honestly, I don't know. This is my first book deal. I'm not sure how it works. We chatted, we left the restaurant, and we started walking back to her office. It was busy, since I mean, it was the financial district toward the end of lunch. Everyone was polite, but you know how it is. At one point I realized Ellie wasn't next to me anymore, so I looked back. She was clutching her stomach, there was blood everywhere, and she collapsed."

"Did you go see if she was okay?"

"Immediately. I rolled her over, and before I had a chance to do anything else, someone nudged me out of the way and told me they were a nurse. I figured they had a better chance than I did at saving her, so I got up and looked around. I saw someone in a dark green hoodie and black sweats running away from the scene, and I gave chase. I almost caught up to them, but they cut across a passing cable car and jumped on. By the time I realized they were on the cable car, it was too late. I called out to the conductor, but they didn't hear me, and there was no way I'd be able to catch it."

"A cable car? Where was it going?"

"Um, up California Street."

Detective Morello wrote that down.

"After that, I went back to where Ellie had been stabbed, and it was already over. She was dead. You were called, and you know the rest."

"Can you describe the person you chased any further? Gender? Age? Height? Build? Race?"

"I only ever saw them from the back. They turned a couple of times, but there were always people in between us; I never saw their face. Given the baggy clothing, I couldn't make out any identifying features. Just that they were probably somewhere between five six and six feet tall. Believe me, I wish I had more to give you."

"Did Ellie mention anyone who had issues with her? An ex-boyfriend, maybe?"

"Nothing of the sort."

Detective Morello asked a few more questions, but it quickly became obvious he didn't know anything.

"Can I see the footage you've got of the murder?" I asked.

He shook his head. "No, sorry. Your attorney has seen it; it was the only way she agreed to have you come speak with me. But I can't go showing it to just anyone."

Read Between the Lies

I nodded. Honestly, that was fair enough. "All right. I hope you find the killer."

"Thank you. And if you remember anything else—even if you don't think it's important—please, let me know."

"I will."

Of course, there was the math competition. Ophelia didn't mention keeping that to myself, but frankly, I figured in this case the police could only harm our chances of finding the other competitors. After all, Mia had pointed a can of pepper spray at us just for being in the vicinity of the clue. I imagined the police presence wouldn't be subtle, and they wouldn't be welcome.

Detective Morello said goodbye, and Sameen and I headed to the elevator.

"Should I have told him about the stuff Ophelia and I found out?" I asked her when the doors closed behind us.

"Did she tell you to?"

I shook my head. "Didn't say either way."

"In that case, she trusts you to use your best judgement. The fact that you didn't mention it tells me you thought that was best."

"Yeah, I think I do. This case is weird already."

"Welcome to life with Ophelia. Sometimes, she takes on run-of-the-mill murders because she's been hired to do it. But when it comes to cases she takes herself, she only ever takes the weird ones. The ones that sound like they wouldn't be out of place in a

Sherlock Holmes casebook. They're interesting, if nothing else."

"I'm starting to see that. Even in this case, there's already a whole wide world out there that I didn't know existed. Math competitions. Ellie might have been killed by a fellow competitor. It's wild."

Sameen grinned. "I know. It's one of the reasons why I love working for Ophelia. I never know what's going to land on my desk, but I know if nothing else, it's going to be interesting."

The doors opened, and we were let back out into the lobby. Sameen and I headed outside, and she said goodbye to me, heading down to the parking garage to grab her car. I was about to pull out my phone to text Ophelia when she pulled up in front of me in her Audi, motioning for me to get in.

I slipped into the passenger side.

"How did it go?"

"Well enough," I replied, hoisting my shoulder upward. "Detective Morello was slightly more polite than the last time I saw him, but his bedside manner could still use a bit of work. He wouldn't show me the video of the stabbing."

"That's all right; I'm sure we'll be able to find it. I was able to get Oliver Dorchester's address; what do you say we pay him a visit?"

"Sounds like a plan. Hopefully we'll get some answers, or at least an indication as to who might have wanted Ellie dead."

"That's what I'm hoping for. I also spoke with

Anthony again. I sent him the image Mia gave us, the original advertisement inviting players to this competition, but he was unable to identify its creator. I'm thinking perhaps we should try to get Fiona on this case."

The corner of my mouth curved upwards. "I don't know. It might interfere with this week's PTA meeting."

"I'm sure she'll claim something. But last week was the first time in a long time that she got to put her real skills to the test, and now that she's gotten a taste of it, I'm sure she'll be more than happy to help. Or at the very least, with a bit of arm-twisting, she'll reluctantly agree."

"That sounds more like it."

Oliver Dorchester lived in Cow's Hollow, in a beige row house with a terra-cotta roof and a bay window jutting out from the second floor. Ophelia knocked on the front door, and about thirty seconds later, a woman in her early twenties answered. She had big blue eyes and thick, curly red hair that added to her already tall frame. Her lips were full and painted fire-engine red. Freckles dotted her cheeks. She was dressed casually, in jean shorts and a white tank top with a blue cardigan over it.

"Hello," she greeted us, a slight note of confusion in her voice.

"Hi. I'm Ophelia Ellis, from Ellis and Associates, and this is my partner, Poppy Perkins. We're looking to speak with Oliver Dorchester."

"Ellis and Associates… are you lawyers?"

"No. Investigative Consultants. Someone Oliver knew was murdered today in town, and we're looking into the case. His name was given as someone who might know the victim, and we're hoping we might learn more about her from him."

The woman's eyes narrowed. "So you don't suspect him?"

"No. We're really just trying to gather information. Is he available?"

"Who was murdered?"

"A woman named Ellie Jacobs."

The hardness in the woman's face immediately disappeared. "Ellie? Are you serious? She's dead?"

"Yes."

"Oh my God, please come in," the woman said, stepping back and holding the door open. When we walked in, she closed it behind us. "Oliver is upstairs. I know he'll want to talk to you. I'm Steph, by the way. His girlfriend."

Steph led the way up the stairs and into an open-concept living room, dining room, and kitchen, which was frankly a little bit rare here in downtown San Francisco. The older houses usually came with older floor plans, which meant completely separate living spaces. But here, the interior walls had been removed. The style was very much Scandinavian minimalist. The dark hardwood floors were covered with a white rug to brighten the space. On one side of the room, a low

Read Between the Lies

shelf, rectangular with round corners, held a few chess-themed books, with a wall-mounted television above it and a red vase in the corner. Across from the TV was a low-to-the-floor white fabric couch, with a round wooden coffee table in front of it. On top were a few books, and I checked out the titles.

Zurich International Chess Tournament 1953.
Chess Informants.
Alekhine's Best Games.

To the left was a dining room, with a laptop on one of the tables. The chair behind it was draped with a dark red hoodie. In one corner of it, in small white lettering were the letters MIT, designed in creative solid rectangles.

Behind that was a modern, elegant kitchen, all glossy and white.

"Oliver," Steph called out, motioning for Ophelia and me to take a seat on the couch. "Can you come out here, please?"

A few seconds later, a man came down the stairs, a slight scowl on his face. He looked like he'd just walked out of a Ralph Lauren ad. Wearing slim-fitting, dark blue jeans and an argyle sweater, his short brown hair was tousled, but it stayed in place so perfectly as he moved that I knew the effect was done on purpose. His blue eyes were icy, his gaze strong as he met mine. I felt an instinctive urge to recoil. His cheekbones were high, his thin lips pressed tight to his mouth, and when he spoke, he had a high English accent, as if he'd just returned from a meeting with the king at Buckingham Palace.

I also couldn't help but notice he stood just a shade under six feet tall.

"Ophelia Ellis," he said, stepping across to the other side of the room and taking a seat at one of the dining chairs while he looked at us. "My father told me about you."

"MI6," Ophelia replied. "I knew the name Dorchester was familiar."

"He'll be disappointed to hear it; he makes an effort to be as forgettable as possible."

"I have an excellent memory."

I didn't know what was going on here, but I knew MI6 was the British equivalent of the CIA, thanks to a childhood spent watching James Bond movies.

"What can I do for you?"

"We have some bad news. A friend of yours, Ellie Jacobs, was murdered this afternoon."

I watched Oliver's reaction carefully, but there wasn't one. He simply stared at Ophelia, his gaze getting even more intense for a few seconds before he spoke. "Ellie? Murdered?"

Ophelia nodded. "Yes. Poppy and I are investigating, and we were told the two of you were friends. We're hoping you can tell us something that could lead us in the direction of her killer."

"Fuck!" Oliver suddenly shouted, slamming his fist down on the dining table, making the whole thing shudder. "No. This can't be right. She can't be dead," he said, rubbing his hands up and down his face. "No, no, no."

Oliver reached over the table, grabbed the salt-shaker from the center of it, and hurled it toward the wall. I watched, riveted, as the porcelain grinder —a very modern set, obviously designer-made— arced across the room before smashing against the wall on the other side and exploding into a million pieces.

Maybe Oliver Dorchester was more of a suspect than I thought.

Chapter 5

Steph rushed to the kitchen. "I'm just going to make everyone a cup of tea," she muttered.

"If your father has told me about you, then you know what it is I do."

"Even Dad didn't know that," Oliver said with a scoff.

"You know enough to know I'm dangerous, though. So, when I told you Ellie was just murdered, and you responded with violence, you had to know who you were talking to."

"So what?" Oliver roared, causing me to jump. "This isn't about you! It's not about me. It's about Ellie. Tell me what happened to her. Now!"

"She was walking downtown today, heading back to the office after lunch. She was stabbed in the street, where she bled out. I'm sorry."

"Damn it," Oliver said, burying his face in his

hands, then smacking the table. "Damn it, it's all over now. Ellie. She's dead."

"I'm going to need you to rein it in, Oliver. I know that temper is what gets you so much attention in the chess world, but right now, Ellie is dead, and I need to know what I can about her. So let's start with this. How well did you know her?"

"We met in undergrad," Oliver replied, his elbows on his knees and his head in his hands. I had to strain to hear the muffled sound of his voice. "We were both math majors. On different tracks, but we'd each attracted attention in our own ways. I was a Grandmaster; I earned the title at seventeen. And she was a math prodigy. People would whisper about the Fields Medal and the Abel as she walked past them, even then. We understood each other."

"Was your relationship romantic?"

"Not at first. We tried dating a little bit. It didn't work out. We were better friends than partners. And then she quit math, and we split apart for a while. We lost touch. I didn't know she was in the city, but a little over two months ago I ran into her by chance at the grocery store."

"You have to admit, your reaction then was a bit strong for someone who claims Ellie was just a friend."

"Oh, Oliver isn't cheating on me or anything," Steph said, coming back over from the kitchen with a mug for him. A teabag hung from the edge. She placed it on a coaster in front of him and stood behind him, rubbing his back gently.

After what he'd done with the saltshaker, I wasn't sure it was the smartest idea ever to put a steaming mug of boiling liquid in front of him, but Oliver wrapped his hands around it and took a careful sip.

"I'm not," Oliver said. "But I can't tell you why I'm upset."

"You have to," Steph said to him softly. "I know you want to keep it a secret, but Ellie's been murdered. You need to tell them."

"We're already aware of the competition Ellie entered, if that's what you're talking about. Is it safe to assume you're also vying for the million-dollar prize?" Ophelia asked.

"It's more than that," Oliver said dully, glancing into the mug. "We were working together to solve it."

"Isn't that sort of collaboration against the rules?" I asked. "After all, the company behind it doesn't want a team. They want one person."

"Yeah. And as far as anyone knew, I was that one person. Ellie wanted to compete, but she didn't want the attention. She came to me and asked for my help. If I went out to find the clues and came to her with the math, she would solve the problems. That was when we got back in touch, about two months ago. I agreed. We would split the prize money. I would go find the clues and bring them back to her, and she would solve them."

"Why?" I asked. "You're the third-best chess player in the world. I have to assume there's money in that. You don't look like you're on poor street."

"There is," Oliver admitted. "A lot of it, even. I made around eight hundred grand last year from tournaments alone, and I have a few endorsement deals. But my chess rankings have dropped. Last year, I was number two in the world. Then that bitch Mayer jumped me in the rankings. I had a few bad games, and she had some good ones. People started talking, asking if I was cooked. And there were, I'm sad to say, some cheating accusations. They're all false, obviously. I might be a lot of things, but I'm not a cheater. If I was, I'd be ranked number one in the world, obviously. It's just morons who are jealous of my standings whispering behind my back. But I'm not an idiot. I know what whispers mean. It's sponsorships drying up. It's fewer tournament invites. I wasn't about to turn down that kind of money, especially not when it just involved hunting down a few clues here and there."

"Still, it's affecting Oliver," Steph said. "It's one thing to know you're better than everyone else. But to have people claim that you didn't get where you are fairly? It's gross. He shouldn't put up with it."

Oliver reached a hand up to his shoulder and placed it on Steph's. "She's right. It is gross, but it is what it is. When Ellie came to me with the proposal,

I figured I could come out of it on top too. If I could win, then it would shut the haters up. I'd prove that my chess skills come from my math background, not from cheating."

"And you were going to prove that by cheating your way through the competition."

"Look, I know that's how it appears, but it's not like that. I was helping. Ellie was just… Even years after she left math, she was just so good. She had a way with numbers. You know how when you see an athlete who's incredible at their sport, they just make it look so easy? That was Ellie but with math. She made the numbers dance for her. She held them in the palm of her hand, and she played with them, like it was the easiest thing in the world. I've never seen anything like it."

"Why did she leave the math world, then? If she was so good, so prodigious?"

Oliver scoffed. "Men. What else? The math world—and the chess world—is full of incels who spent their entire childhoods indoors with their faces buried in a book and never learned how to talk to a woman. Then they hit college, they think they're entitled to sex, they become huge creeps, and then people wonder why women are driven out of these programs in droves. Ellie had a classmate who sexually assaulted her. When nobody did anything about it after she reported it, she decided she had enough. She left the program. Not that I can blame her."

"And she went into English?" I asked.

"Yeah. I think it was the opposite of what she was used to doing, which is why. Ellie never really liked the attention she got being a math prodigy. We were different that way. Me? I live for it. But she just wanted to lock herself up in her room, do her problems, and come back out with the solutions later. That's why this worked out so well. I could go and get the clues, I'd send them to her, she could work on them on her own time, and she didn't have to do anything else. Even now, even after all this time away, she was so good. She was so creative. She could see things in the numbers that other people wouldn't notice. But I guess that's all ruined now. I'm not going to get any more answers from her."

"Pity," Ophelia replied, her tone making it obvious she didn't think it was a pity at all.

"You don't get it," Oliver said, shaking his head. "You don't get it at all. You're not famous, like me. When you get to this level, there's pressure like you wouldn't believe. You think doing stuff with MI6 is hard? That's nothing when you see your name in the paper, accused of being a cheater in one sentence while they wonder if you're better than Bobby Fisher the next. I had to do this. And I'm sad that Ellie is dead, because she was a very good friend. But it also does make my life more difficult."

"And what do you think of all this?" I asked Steph, who was still standing behind her boyfriend.

She shook her head sadly. "It's awful, really. I knew Oliver was working with Ellie again. I thought it would be a good thing. You should see the things that are said about him, and they're all lies. If he could have won that competition, it would have been so good for him. But now there's no chance."

"How long have the two of you been together?" I asked.

"About six months, this time around," Oliver said. "We dated a couple of years ago and broke up but found each other again."

"Can you think of anyone who could have wanted to hurt Ellie?" Ophelia asked. "Did she mention anybody? Did she have a boyfriend?"

Oliver shook his head. "No. She was single; I do know that. Ellie was reserved. She was like a lot of great mathematicians; she was an introvert. She preferred to spend her Friday nights indoors, working on her stuff. She could turn on the charm when she needed to, no question about it, but at the end of the day, she liked to keep company with her own brain rather than with other people. I don't know of anyone who would have wanted to hurt her. She didn't mention anybody."

"So if you're saying you were the one who went to find all of the clues, no one else from the math competition could have known she was involved, right?" I asked. "Unless they somehow found out about the two of you working together."

"That's right. There's no way anyone else could have known. I didn't tell anyone apart from Steph."

"And I only know people in the math world

through Oliver," Steph replied with a shrug. "It's not my world. I work in advertising sales."

"So unless Ellie told somebody what we were doing—and she wouldn't have; she understood how important discretion was—there's no way anybody could have known about her role in this," Oliver said. "She had to be killed over something else."

"Do you know anybody else who is involved in the competition?"

"No. I was always careful when I went to collect clues, making sure nobody spotted me. I wanted my win to come as a surprise to everybody involved. I didn't want it leaked in advance that Oliver Dorchester was competing in a math scavenger hunt. I wanted to stun everyone when I finally won. So I took precautions. Besides, with Ellie helping me with the math, I'm pretty sure we were in first place."

"I can confirm there's at least one person who was very close on your heels."

Oliver swore. "Well, I guess it doesn't matter anymore anyway. It's not like I'd be able to win it on my own."

"What were you going to do about the prize, if you won?" I asked. "After all, there's a million dollars and a job on offer. You said you were going to split they money, right?"

"Yeah, that was our deal. Half and half. She could flex her math muscles again behind the scenes, without knowing anyone was involved. And it's not like I wasn't helping at all. We worked together on the puzzles. She told me she'd figured out the latest one. She was trying to find coordinates using the Goldbach Conjecture."

"She was," Ophelia confirmed, nodding.

"So we were going to split the money, and I would turn down the job offer, telling the company that while it was very good of them, and I'd be honored, blah, blah, blah, I already had a career that I was devoted to, and that maybe after I became the best chess player in the world and tired of that I'd come work for them. Boilerplate stuff, you understand?"

"Ellie didn't plan on revealing herself and taking the job, then?" I asked.

"No. Of course not. For one thing, both of us would be immediately disqualified. No working in teams. But Ellie also actually liked her job. She mentioned it a lot. She didn't want to go back into math permanently. She just liked the challenge of being involved behind the scenes."

"Did she mention anyone at her job? Anyone she was having trouble with?"

"Trouble? No, I'm not sure I'd say that. She did clash with her boss a little bit, but that's rather to be expected, I think. The woman was tough. She expected Ellie to get more work done than she could manage, and Ellie did her best to fight back and argue that to make the best books possible, she needed more time on each manuscript. But it was a regular workplace disagreement between employer and employee. It's certainly not the sort of thing one would kill over."

"You would be very surprised to hear some of the reasons people kill," Ophelia pointed out.

"I suppose I would. It's so uncivilized, really. One expects a certain level of violence when one moves to America, but to have it happen to someone like Ellie is really unconscionable."

"Why did you move here?" I asked.

"The opportunities to train are better in this country. Four of the top ten players in the world right now are American. And the energy is different here. In San Francisco in particular. There's an undercurrent of self-determination in this city. It's a city full of people with ambition. And I don't simply mean making money. For some, that is the goal, yes. But for others, it's to make the world a better place. To fight climate change. To create art that speaks to people. The glue that binds this city is that unrelenting energy to keep moving forward, and that suits me, because I'm the same way. I'm going to be the best chess player in the world, and there's nobody that's going to stop me."

"England wasn't quite doing that for you?"

Oliver scoffed. "No. England is full of self-important, pompous gits who think the family you were born into determines how good of a person you are. No matter what you do with yourself, there's always going to be people above you who believe you should be stomped on just because you didn't happen to win the lottery of souls upon your birth. And I say that as someone who was born into a good family, just not one with a title that can be traced back to the Lancastrian kings. I went to Eton. I know all of those types, and let me tell you, just because you're third in line to inherit a title doesn't make you any less of a twat. It's an attitude that will drive that country into the ground if it doesn't change, quite frankly. So, I moved here, where judgements are made based on who you are, not what you were born into. And my life has very much improved for it. Your environment affects who you are and how you act. You must believe that as well, given as you've moved here."

"To an extent, I do," Ophelia replied. "A true meritocracy is certainly preferable to an oligarchic system where only a few are capable of succeeding."

"So that's why I moved here, two years ago."

"And you didn't speak to Ellie before two months ago?"

"No. I didn't realize she was here. I happened to run into her at the Safeway near the Ferry Building a couple of months ago. It was pure chance; I needed some Advil, and she was grabbing some snacks for the office. We exchanged numbers then and texted a couple of times, and when she texted me to ask if I'd be willing to help shield her identity as she competed in the maths thing, I agreed."

"Is there anything else that you think could help us find Ellie's killer?"

"Not that I know of. But speak to the people at her work. They might know more. Ellie was dedicated to her job, and if anything was going on with her, I bet it was there. You're sure this wasn't a random thing?"

Ophelia shrugged. "It can't be ruled out entirely, of course, but I'm leaning toward no. I'm certainly investigating it as if it were a targeted murder. If it wasn't, we're left with only physical evidence in trying to hunt down the killer, and that is the kind of grunt work the police have far more resources to draw upon than me."

"I just hope you find the person who did this," Steph said. She was obviously a fidgeter; she grabbed the hoodie that hung off the back of the dining chair where Oliver was seated and hung it up in a closet next to the stairs, then moved to the kitchen and started folding dishtowels as she watched on. "Poor Ellie. I didn't know her very well; I only met her a couple of times when she came here to work with Oliver, but she was nice. Very pleasant."

"In that case, I ask this only to rule you out as a suspect, but can you tell me where you were this afternoon, around one o'clock?"

Oliver looked like he wanted to argue for a moment but then thought better of it, pursing his lips. "I was here. Working. Alone. From eight in the morning to eight at night, I work upstairs in my office. Studying chess moves. I don't like distractions."

"You weren't here?" I asked Steph.

"No. I work a regular nine-to-five, so I was in the office."

"I didn't do this, though. I never would have done this. I liked Ellie. I wanted that boost to my reputation that could help me in the chess world, and she was the only reason I had a chance at it. I'm good at math, but not that good. It's over for me. It's not going to ruin my life or anything, but it would have given me some good press at a time when that would have been handy. And of course, the extra money in my bank account wouldn't have hurt, either."

"You have to admit, there's a saltshaker over there that shows you're not the best at handling your emotions," Ophelia said. "And I do have access to the internet. I know your history. The game in Mexico City last year?"

"I made a mistake," Oliver said with a sigh. "It wasn't good of me. It was not sportsmanlike. But you know what? This is the sort of thing that happens when you strive to be the best. So I've got a little bit of a temper sometimes. I've been working on it. But lots of people have tempers. That doesn't make them all killers."

"You drove a chef's knife into the center of a chessboard after you lost," Ophelia said, her voice hard. "That's a little bit more than losing your temper, don't you think? You had to bring that knife in with you to that match."

"I said it was a mistake, all right?" Oliver said, his voice rising. "I wasn't in a good place in Mexico City. I let my nerves get the better of me, in what was an important match that would determine a lot."

"It was the match after which Mayer took over second place in the world rankings, if I remember correctly?"

"Yes. That's right. Anna is not half the chess player I am."

"And yet she beat you the last time you faced one another," Ophelia said, her stare hard.

"She did, because I wasn't on my game. I let the pressure get to me. Do you think I haven't analyzed that game a thousand times? I had four opportunities that I let slip past me that could have won me that game. I'm not mad at her. She's not as good a chess player as I am. I'm angry with myself for not taking advantage of the opportunity and for letting her pass me."

"You called her a bitch when Ophelia first mentioned her," I pointed out.

"Because she is a bitch. Uppity Austrian who thinks she's better than everyone else. I shouldn't have stabbed the board after she beat me, okay? But I did it. It was a mistake. It doesn't mean I killed Ellie. I liked Ellie. I don't like Anna. There's a big difference. I didn't kill her. Look into my life all you want. I'm serious."

Ophelia nodded. "All right, thank you. We appreciate your time. Can I get your phone number, so that if anything else comes up I can contact you again?"

"Yes, of course. Anything that I can do to help you find whoever did this to Ellie," Oliver replied, his voice still terse and cold. Steph went to the kitchen, pulled a set of Post-it notes from a drawer, and handed them to him. Oliver jotted down his phone number then tore off the note and passed it to Ophelia.

"Thank you."

"I'll walk you out," Steph said, and we followed her back downstairs. She paused as she opened the door. "He didn't do it. You have to understand that. He was working *with* Ellie. There were no problems between the two of them. If there were, he would have told me. We tell each other everything. He needed her. He desperately wanted the good publicity that would come from winning that competition—and the money. He wouldn't have killed her. I'm telling you."

"Thanks, Steph," Ophelia said with a smile. "We'll keep that in mind. We're not on a witch hunt here. We're just trying to get to the truth."

"And that is the truth. Oliver wouldn't have done this. I'm the girlfriend who knows him better than anyone, believe me. I live with him. If he had done this, I would be the first to give him up."

The two of us left and climbed back into Ophelia's car. Night had fallen; it was getting late.

"What do you think?" Ophelia asked me as we drove toward Chinatown, where she would drop me off at my building.

I frowned. "It's hard to know. He's obviously got a temper, and the fact that he used a knife to stab a chessboard a few months ago isn't a great look."

"No. I remember the incident well; it caused quite a bit of a stir in the chess world."

"While I think he could be the killer, my question would be why? What's his motive? After all, if he's telling us the truth, and he was working with Ellie, he would have had no reason to kill her. Her death actually complicates his life, since it makes it impossible for him to win that prize."

"Indeed, that is the question, isn't it?" Ophelia said pensively.

"That said, I certainly think he should be a suspect, even if he wasn't when we went in there. The incident with the knife in Mexico City only seals it. Ellie was stabbed with a knife too. And he has no alibi."

"Yes, I agree. He is on the list of suspects for sure. I would like to know who's behind the maths competition. There's nothing more we can do today. Come into the office tomorrow, and we'll see what we can uncover."

"Sounds good. I can be there around nine."

"Perfect."

Ophelia dropped me off in front of my apartment building, and I headed upstairs, my mind whirring. Had Oliver killed Ellie? And if so, why? What could have happened between them that would have led to him wanting to murder her?

Chapter 6

I WOKE UP THE NEXT MORNING TO A TEXT FROM Jenny, my former coworker at San Techcisco Donuts, also known as STD.

Hi, Poppy. Is there a chance you can come by the shop? I wanted to have a chat with you and see how you're doing. And offer you your old job back. Anyway, I'm here now, and I'll be around all day, so if you're interested, stop by anytime.

Jenny finished the message with a smiling emoji, and I pursed my lips as I stared at the phone. On the one hand, I had some pretty terrible memories of that place. On the other, it sounded like Jenny had taken over the store. And I had no doubt that she, unlike her aunt, would be a good boss. Someone I'd want to work under.

Cool. I'll be there soon.

Despite trying to avoid it, my stomach did a little bit of a nervous flip-flop. What was going on with STD? Jenny had just told me that she was going to offer me my old job back. But did I *want* my old job back? It certainly would make things easier for me if I did. The end of the month was fast approaching, and my rent was going to come due. I still didn't have a new roommate. Not that I'd really put a lot of effort into finding one. It was amazing how quickly the days were taken up when you'd gotten stabbed not all that long ago.

At least thanks to the initial deposit from Leon Books, my bank account had more than a single-digit quantity of money in it. I could afford a couple of months of paying for this place by myself without worrying about impending homelessness, but I still had to get onto the roommate thing. And I had to find another job.

It was just after eight in the morning. I had told Ophelia I would be at her office at nine, and STD was on the way, so I quickly threw on some clothes, had a quick look at the weather forecast to make sure I wasn't going to be dressed totally inappropri-ately—I had never lived in a city where the weather could be so variable, even among individual neigh-borhoods—then headed downstairs to LLB Coffee.

Located on the ground floor of the building, LLB Coffee was owned by two of my favorite people in the world. Lily and Laura Belle were the married couple who ran this place and had done so since the late eighties. Over the years, they had carved themselves out a nice little niche by growing a reputation of making quality coffee, offering the most delicious pastries east of Nob Hill, and making sure the service had more small-town charm than big-city business.

I stepped inside to find the place already humming with activity. The tables at the back were taken up by a group of locals, enjoying a cup of tea while speaking excitedly to one another. Near the windows were a couple of students, books propped open and tapping away at laptops, already into another big day. The line consisted mainly of people grabbing a takeaway cup of joe and maybe a couple of Laura Belle's famous beignets on the way to the office.

I joined the line, and when I got to the front, I was met with a wide smile from Lily. "Good morning, Poppy. How's the shoulder?"

"It's slowly getting better," I replied. "Although yesterday I had to chase a murderer, and that didn't exactly help."

"No, I can't imagine it would have. What are you doing, going around chasing murderers again? I thought all that was over."

"Different murder."

"The one down near the Ferry Building?" I nodded. "I heard about that."

"It was my editor. I had just been meeting with her for lunch."

"Oh, you're joking!"

"I wish I was. I didn't catch them, though. They jumped on a cable car and got away."

"Well, it's a good effort to even get close to them with one arm. I'm sorry about your editor."

"Thanks."

"What's going to happen now with your contract?"

I shrugged. "I'm not sure yet. I guess they'll assign me someone else, but that hasn't happened yet. Of course, the company has some bigger priorities right now. I'm going to keep writing as much as I can of this book, and then when I get assigned someone else, I'll start working with them."

"I'm glad you're being sensible about it. That does explain Juliette, though."

"She was here?" I asked, pressing my lips together. Deep down, I wanted to be the bigger person. I wanted to move on from that relationship and be able to say that her existence had no effect on me. But to my core, I was petty and a hater, and the sound of her name made my insides smolder with rage.

"About two hours ago, right after we opened. She beat the morning rush; I think she wanted to have some time with me alone. Came in with her eyes watering, like she'd just been crying, and she put on a big show of being upset."

I rolled my eyes. "She was willing to dump this place like Andy dumped Woody when he got Buzz Lightyear, but the instant she thought she could get some attention, she was back."

"Exactly. I hadn't seen her in days. She kept

glancing at me while I was punching her order in, like she couldn't figure out why I wasn't asking her what was wrong. She sniveled a few times, too, for good measure. Then, she told me she was having a horrible day, and I replied by telling her the total came to four seventeen."

I cackled. "I bet she didn't like that."

"No," Lily said with a grin. "She told me I'd obviously been conned by you and that you were a lying bitch. She went on a little bit along those same lines and then told me she was never coming back here again, since I obviously didn't care about her."

"Ah, yes, there's nothing Juliette can't make about herself. Honestly, I feel like an idiot for not seeing it sooner. I should have recognized she was a self-absorbed moron long before she stole my book idea."

Lily shrugged. "It's hard when you're close to people, especially when they change over time. I didn't know Juliette in undergrad, but I wouldn't be surprised if she wasn't like this then."

"Yeah. You're right about that; she wasn't."

"Anyway, she got her coffee and flipped me off as she left, shaking her head. I think she wanted to be the one to tell me about your editor's murder."

"I wonder if we shared the same one," I mused. "She never told me who was working with her."

"Not your monkey, not your circus," Lily said as I pulled out my card and pressed it against the small white card reader. "You've got your own book to think about. Deal with that."

"You're right. As always. Mom always said my vengeful streak would get me into trouble one day."

"It will, but sometimes people deserve it too."

"I'll keep that in mind," I said with a smile. "Thanks, Lily. Have a good one, okay?"

"You too."

I slipped down the counter to where John, one of the regular baristas who worked here, was busy steaming milk, the low whirr of hot air frothing up the milk in his metal jug a comforting sound. I leaned against the wall next to the bathroom. So Juliette had come here looking for sympathy. I knew I should just let it go. Let her go. Mom would tell me that you can't take things like that personally. You have to focus on yourself.

And I knew, deep down, that she was right. But Juliette had wronged me, and not only that—now that I'd cut her out of my life, she was still coming to these places to try to get attention, attention for something that actually affected *me*. I had been there. I was the one who turned and saw the blood flowing from Ellie's abdomen. I was the one who had chased the killer in the green hoodie. Not her.

Taking a deep breath, I closed my eyes. If Juliette was that desperate for attention, let her be. Lily was right. I had to take care of my own life. Right now, that meant heading down to San Techcisco Donuts and having that conversation with Jenny.

Located in a small shop on the outskirts of Union Square, I was surprised to arrive at San Techcisco donuts to find the front windows covered in newspaper, not allowing anyone to look in.

I knocked on the front door, and a couple of seconds later heard the familiar click of the lock. Jenny greeted me with a smile and let me in. Standing around my height and on the slimmer side, Jenny was dressed casually in loose jeans and a grey T-shirt stained white with paint. She had on a pair of Converse sneakers. Her chestnut-brown hair was tied back in a ponytail, with her bangs and random loose wisps of hair framing her makeup-free face.

"Poppy," she said, greeting me warmly as she let me in. "Come on inside. I want you to check this out."

I stepped into the store and my mouth dropped open as I looked around. "Oh, wow. You're redoing this whole place."

STD had been one of those glossy, clean, crisp establishments designed to basically be the food version of an Apple Store. Now, though, there was so much more to it. The glossy plastic counter where everyone worked was gone. So was the linoleum floor; I was now standing on lightly stained pale hardwood. The paper-white walls had been painted a light shade of pastel pink.

The old white shelves behind the counter that were used for storage had been removed and replaced with open gold metal frames with glass shelving.

"Incredible," I gasped, my eyes taking in the whole scene. "Jenny, this looks great."

"Thanks," my former coworker said from the front of the store, looking around and beaming. "I've put so much work into this place over the past week. How are you doing? How's your shoulder?"

I instinctively reached out and touched it. "Getting better. I've been keeping up with my physio. I'll live, thanks to you."

Jenny waved a hand. "No, not thanks to me. Thanks to modern medicine. I just helped get you to the car. And did what Ophelia told me."

"So, what's going on here? Do you own this place now?"

"I do. The last week has been completely wild. Elana decided to sell, of course. She wanted to get rid of any memories of this place. I didn't think I would have the cash to manage it, and then somehow, I woke up the next day, and I got a call from someone from one of those finance companies. They had heard what happened, and they wanted to offer me a loan at prime, and that they had already spoken with Elana. She would sell me the coffee shop for two hundred and fifty grand. I agreed, and that afternoon there was three hundred grand sitting in my bank account. I literally thought it was a mistake. Like, they meant to go to someone else. You know how you read about that happening sometimes? I was going to call the bank and be like, 'Uhhh, can you take this money out of my account before I spend it and you come after me and sue me?' But I had all the documents, they were signed, the loan was legit. I could buy this place."

"That's wild."

"Yeah. I still don't have a freaking clue where that money came from beyond the company name. But you know what? I'm not about to ask too many questions about it. So, I called Elana, and sure enough, she named her price at two fifty and said she wasn't going to negotiate it down further. That was fine with me. I told her I'd take it. She was suspicious at first. She didn't know where I'd gotten the money, and you know what she's like. Always putting her nose where it doesn't belong. Well, I told her to pound sand and that she could either sell it to me at the price she named, or she could spend months trying to offload her murder shop to someone else. She agreed, she signed the papers, and now this place is mine. It's official."

"And you're changing it up?"

"One hundred percent. That's what the other fifty grand is going toward. For one thing, I'm changing the name. Literally the first thing. I haven't figured out what I'm changing it to, but anything is better than San Techcisco Donuts. Okay, maybe not *anything*. I'm not calling it Chlamydia Crème."

"Nuts in the Hole?" I suggested with a grin.

Jenny burst out laughing. "Dippin' Dick's Donuts."

"The O-Zone."

"Oh yeah, even better. I can't believe Elana never saw STD as being a bad name. And San Techcisco by itself sucks. I don't know what I'm changing this place's name to, but I guarantee you it will not be suggestive. Or anything that you can remotely link to something you need to get tested for."

I laughed. "I'm glad to hear that."

"Seriously. How did she go for San Techcisco when San Franciscdough was right there?"

"I mean, Elana doesn't strike me as being the most creative person on the planet."

"No. But it's fine. Now, this place is all mine. The counters are ordered and coming in tomorrow. They're going to be a warm white farmhouse style. Then I'm going to tile the whole back wall in glossy white subway tiles and bring in the tables and chairs, and we'll be able to reopen. I want this place to feel warm and welcoming. This city has enough places that feel sterile. I don't want this to be one of them."

"I think it looks fantastic."

"And so how would you feel about coming back to work here, maybe as assistant manager? I'm hoping to get as much of the old staff back as usual. I already spoke to Oliver and Rosa; they're both going to keep working. But neither one of them are full-time. And I'm going to have to hire at least two more people."

"I don't know," I said slowly. "I honestly haven't really thought about it yet."

"And that's totally fine. I don't want to pressure you. It's not like I'm opening tomorrow anyway. I'm hoping to be ready to go four days from now. And if you aren't ready then, that's cool with me too. But I also want you to know, things will be different under me. For one thing, wages are increasing."

"Oh?"

"Yeah. Elana thought minimum wage was acceptable; I don't. I've run the numbers. I'm going to be increasing the cost of donuts by twenty cents each, and that should bring in enough money to pay everybody twenty-two bucks an hour."

I tried to hide my surprise. Twenty-two dollars an hour? That would be quite the significant raise.

"That's great."

"It's what everyone deserves. It's total bull that Elana thought she could pay people the absolute bare minimum the law required her to, especially in a place like the city, where the cost of living is so high. Like I said, things are going to change here. In all aspects. Elana is my aunt, and I love her, but she was a terrible owner, and I want my employees to feel like they're valued. Like they're more than just a cog in a machine that's designed to churn out money every single day. If you come back to work here, I promise, things are going to be different."

I had always thought Jenny would have made a better manager than her aunt. "Okay, I'm in," I found myself saying. My instincts were that this was a good idea. And frankly, I wasn't about to say no to a significant raise.

A smile broke out across Jenny's face. "You are? Great! I'm so glad to hear it. I was really hoping you'd say that, since I want as much of the old crew around as possible. I'm keeping most of Elana's old recipes, and I'll be adding new ones, but I need people who know how to actually make the donuts."

"Yeah. Whatever you need, I'm here. Although I will add that I got a book contract."

"You did?" Jenny squealed. "Why didn't you open with that? Congratulations!"

"Thanks," I said, warmth climbing up the back of my neck. I wasn't really used to people congratulating me on this yet; so far, I'd only told Laura Belle and Lily.

"When do you publish?"

"About a year from now. Next January is the date."

"That's amazing!"

"Thanks. Don't tell anyone; it's not supposed to be public until next week. But seeing as you're my boss, I figured I should tell you, since I might have to schedule around meetings and things like that."

"Of course. It's not a problem at all. I totally

understand. It would be great if you could give me as much notice as possible on those things, so I can try to schedule other people around you—I don't want the others to find themselves accidentally swamped—but I get it, and whenever you need to meet with your book people, that's fine with me."

"Thanks, Jenny. I appreciate it." And I did. It was nice to have a boss who was willing to work around my other job. My new career.

It still felt weird to say it that way, but that's what it was.

"It's going to be nice to have you back. How long are you going to be in the sling?"

"Another two weeks or so, if everything goes according to plan."

"Okay, cool. I'll organize things so you'll have to use your arm as little as possible."

"Thanks. Do you know who sent you the money to buy this place?"

Jenny shook her head. "Not a clue in the world. It's weird, isn't it? But then I guess everything that had to do with that Jason Bergman case was weird. He was so famous; it was all over the news. Maybe it was one of our regulars. There are enough ultra-rich people in this town. It kind of had to be one of them, didn't it? I guess I just have to hope that it was done entirely out of the goodness of their hearts and that I'm not going to get another letter in the mail at some point telling me they now own my soul."

I chuckled nervously. "I hope not."

"I don't think there's a huge risk of that happening," Jenny said with a grin. "When I heard Elana was selling, I manifested this. I asked the universe for help, and it came through for me. I'm not going to ask too many questions about the details."

"Good call. Okay, I'll leave you to it, because I have to go meet a friend at nine o'clock too. It was nice seeing you, Jenny. I love what you've done here."

"Thanks. I'll be in touch. As I said, I'm hoping to open in four days."

"I should be available."

I said goodbye to Jenny and headed back out onto the street, a little perk in my step. Jenny was going to be a great owner. And now one of my problems was completely sorted out: I had my old job back.

And with a significant raise too. Things were going well. Now it was time to help Ophelia find the killer.

Chapter 7

I walked the rest of the way to Ophelia's office, passing by the scene of Ellie's death along the way. I shuddered as I saw the spot on the pavement where she'd died. I couldn't tear my eyes from it.

Time was a funny thing. In this very spot, just yesterday, a woman had lost her life. She'd bled to death right here. And yet now, only twenty-four hours later, there was almost no sign of it. The red bricks of the sidewalk had been cleaned. The yellow police tape that would have barricaded the crime scene was gone. Against the building along which we'd been walking, a small shrine had been established, the only remaining evidence of a tragedy having occurred here recently.

About two dozen bouquets of flowers were propped up against the building a few feet from where Ellie had been killed. They were dotted with cards, candles, messages of support, and more. I swallowed hard as I saw them.

But still, even among the grieving, people continued along. They walked on the same bricks that Ellie had bled on the afternoon before, going about their lives. That was the effect time had. This same spot had been the scene of a tragedy yesterday, but today it was just another path for people to take as they went to work.

I hurried past and headed to Ophelia's office. She was already there, in the conference room, a laptop in front of her when I arrived.

"Good morning," she greeted me. "How are you?"

"Well, I went and saw Jenny at the donut shop, and she gave me my old job back. So that's a plus. And I'm getting a raise. By the way, you wouldn't happen to know how she ended up with that extra cash to do up the place, do you?"

Ophelia shot me a sly look. "Wouldn't have a clue."

"I didn't think so. Well, *whoever* did it, it was very good of them. Jenny is going to be a great owner of that place. She's changing the name."

"I would certainly hope so. What's it going to be called?"

"She's not sure yet. But she's smart. Whatever she decides on will be better than the old name."

"To be fair, that bar is so low it's in the basement."

Read Between the Lies

"Yeah, true. Anyway, I wasn't sure if I was going to take her up on it, but I'm not going to say no to that pay rise. And to be honest, it's easier to go back to working there in a way. The thing about starting a new job is there's always new things to learn. They're not necessarily hard, but it's a lot to handle, mentally."

"Yes, and given as you've already got a lot going on in your life at the moment, it's mental energy you probably don't want to spare right now."

"Exactly. My arm is still in this sling for two more weeks too. I know I can manage with it, but it might make employers a little bit more wary about hiring me right away. Ultimately, this is the right choice, I think. And if it's not, I can handle that challenge when we get to it."

"That's the right attitude."

"And for now, anyway, Jenny is setting up the new store, and I'm focusing on this murder. What are we up to this morning?"

"I texted Fiona, asking her to come when she got the chance, so we're waiting to see if she arrives."

"You have some nerve," a raised voice called out from the elevator.

I raised my eyebrows. "I think she's here."

A moment later, Fiona entered the conference room. About five foot eight, wearing slim black pants, a tight-fitting white shirt, a baby blue jacket over that, and heeled white sandals, Fiona's

85

perfectly coiffed blond hair hung just past her shoulders. A Birkin was on her arm, and she tossed it casually on the table as she stormed toward Ophelia, waving a finger in her face.

"I told you not to contact me again, didn't I? I said I didn't want anything to do with you."

Ophelia stood from her chair and met Fiona head-on. "And yet you're here, aren't you?"

"I was in the city anyway. I had a breakfast, for a charity that I'm on the board of. I figured if I came in here in person, maybe you would get the message. I'm not interested in working for you again. I worked on the Bergman case, because I had my own reasons to want his killer found, but that's all. I'm not your puppy dog, Ophelia. You can't just call and expect me to come running with my tail wagging."

"I know you don't work for me anymore. But I thought perhaps you might enjoy a little bit of freelance work."

"No. No, I don't work anymore. Not for money. I do charity stuff, I take care of my kids, and that's it. I go home to my normal life, my normal husband, my normal children, in my normal house."

"You and I both know there's nothing normal about that house," Ophelia said.

"You know what I mean. It's a real house. I don't live out of a warehouse on the outskirts of

London anymore, rolling out of bed and finding myself at my computer. Goodbye, Ophelia."

"Does that mean you don't even want to know what I want you to do?"

"Nope, I do not," Fiona replied. She grabbed her bag. "Poppy, it's nice to see you again. But if you have any desire at all to live a normal life, I implore you: stay away from Ophelia. She will drag you down into the depths of her crazy life if you let her."

With that, Fiona stormed back out of the room, her heels clicking as she headed back down the hall toward the elevator. I heard a ding, and the doors opened. When they closed again, I turned to Ophelia.

"That didn't really go as well as you expected, did it?"

"Give it a minute," Ophelia replied with a smile.

The two of us sat in silence for about fifteen seconds, and then I heard the sound of the elevator doors open once more. "Out of curiosity," Fiona's voice called out, "what's your target?"

"It's not a straight hack. I need to hunt down who created a certain poster. All I have is a JPG. First the company, then I need a name."

Silence followed for about ten seconds, and then Fiona's heels began clicking on the floor once more. I smiled to myself as she reentered the conference room.

"What do you have? Let me see it."

Ophelia handed Fiona her phone. "You don't have a digital version of it? PDF?"

"No."

"Okay, I can work with this. First step is to track down the original image. Then there's a QR code in the corner. God, I love these things. When they first started being used, around 2007, 2008, or so, they were ahead of their time. No one used them, because no one understood them except nerds. But now that technology has caught up, they're every-where. All you need to do is open your phone camera and scan it, and it'll send you straight to a link. And they're trackable."

"Does that mean you can find out who made it?" I asked.

"It means that at the very least, I can get data on who scanned it. And from there, we'll see what I can find. But that's getting ahead of myself. It's going to be a challenge, especially if I don't have any data on the creator, or even the original poster. Same room as last time?"

"It's ready and set up for you."

"Words cannot express how disgusted I am by you right now," Fiona said as she rose from her chair. "And by myself."

"I told you the last time we met, this is who you are. Embrace it. You will never be truly happy without it, no matter how much you tell yourself otherwise."

"I was truly happy before you steamrolled your

way back into my life," Fiona snapped back. "I have to be finished before noon. Anna is bringing some friends home after school, and I need to have snacks ready."

"I have no doubt you will be finished with this long before then," Ophelia said with another smile.

Fiona shook her head as she walked off. I knew if anyone had a chance of tracking down the creator of that poster, it was her.

"I'm wondering if it's got anything to do with that competition," I said to Ophelia when Fiona left. "After all, Oliver did say he was careful about making sure he wasn't seen. He didn't want anybody to know what he was doing."

"In my experience, when most people say they are very careful about something, they are not nearly as careful as they should be," Ophelia replied. "If you want to follow somebody, you will be inherently more alert to the situation than the person you are following. I do not take him at his word, and I still believe it's very possible someone from the maths competition did this."

"I wanted to look up his cheating scandal," I said, pulling out my phone and tapping away in the search bar. "He's a good suspect, right off the bat. And I'm going to call Leon Books later to see if I've been assigned a new editor. I'm hoping that I can meet some of the people Ellie worked with. Maybe one of them had something against her."

"Good idea," Ophelia said. She had a laptop in

front of her and began tapping away while I read an article on my phone.

The chess world is a small community, and whispers travel fast. There have been rumors over the past few months that the world number three, GM Oliver Dorchester, may have cheated his way into his current Elo score of 2784. While GM Anna Mayer overtook him for the number-two spot recently, that hasn't stopped the questions surrounding GM Dorchester's play over the past year.

The rumors began after the Wijk aan Zee tournament in the Netherlands two years ago, when GM Dorchester upset the world's number one player, GM Abas Benayoun from France. At the time, GM Dorchester was ranked 120th in the world, with an Elo score of 2612. Of course, anybody can have a bad day, and GM Benayoun came out after the day congratulating Dorchester and predicting that his ranking would improve significantly over the coming months.

GM Benayoun was proved correct. In the following year, GM Dorchester's Elo score rose from 2612 to 2720, an increase in a single year that astounded many and had quite a few people asking questions about whether it was possible for someone at that level to increase their skills so rapidly without outside help.

The problem lies in the proof. GM Dorchester has addressed the accusations head-on multiple times, even going so far as to offer to play in a tournament in the nude to discount any possible chance of him hiding a machine on his body that might allow him to cheat.

"Who knows? It could lead to a massive rise in the popularity of chess," GM Dorchester quipped upon making the

suggestion earlier this year. "Maybe we could sell the photos to Playboy."

While GM Dorchester's easy brushing off of the claims against him is enough to many, some in the chess world aren't quite as ready to take him at his word. Behind the scenes, many are still questioning his meteoric rise over the past two years, which Dorchester attributes to a stricter regimen of study and play over that time period.

"Look, the thing is, I was a Grandmaster at seventeen. Sure. But there are over 1700 Grandmasters in the history of chess. Going from that level to becoming one of the best in the world is an entirely different game. I went from studying for four hours a day to studying for eight. I competed in over a hundred matches in the past year. This is where my results are coming from. Anyone who accuses me of cheating is either jealous of me, too small-minded to understand the dedication I've given to this craft, or is simply fond of stirring up drama for drama's sake."

Nonetheless, while no official allegations have been made against GM Dorchester, and no proof of his cheating has ever been offered—despite his games coming under closer scrutiny than most—the rumors persist. Will the truth ever be revealed?

If GM Dorchester is playing fairly, then perhaps only time will reveal him to be an honest actor, given the impossibility of proving a negative. But there are many out there who believe that he is cheating and that one day, he will be caught.

I scrolled back up to the top of the article. The picture featured showed Oliver playing against Anna Mayer, the world number two. According to the caption, this was the match in which she beat him and took over the number-two spot in the world.

I looked at the picture carefully. First, Oliver. There didn't seem to be anything strange in his clothing. He wore slacks and a sweater, not unlike how he'd been dressed the night before. He was in the middle of making a move, having picked up his white bishop. Was it possible he had some electronics underneath his clothes? Sure, but they would have had to be very subtle. Maybe something in his shoes. I checked his ears, too, but saw nothing.

Of course, the people accusing him of cheating had probably done all of this a thousand times over as well. They would have pored over every inch of every photo and video of all the games they had access to, trying to find any sign that Oliver wasn't playing fair.

I moved on and looked at Anna Mayer. She was slim, with an angular face, light brown eyes, and straight, dark-brown hair held back with a white headband. In the photo, she rested her chin on her hand as she eyed the board, focused.

Suddenly, something caught my eye. In the background of the photo, in the crowd. I wasn't one hundred percent sure. After all, the camera's focus was on the two players, not on the people watching. But still…

"Do you think this is Ellie?" I asked Ophelia, getting up and handing her my phone across the table. She took it and carefully looked at the image. The hair color was wrong, since the woman in the photo was blond, but there was a resemblance.

"It's possible. When was this photo taken?"

"Three months ago. When Anna Mayer beat Oliver and took over second place in the world rankings. And Oliver told us he only ran into her two months ago."

"So he did," Ophelia mused. "There is a lot that is interesting about this photo. Good find, Poppy."

Before I had a chance to respond, Fiona reentered the room, a laptop in hand.

"Okay, I've got a whole bunch of information here. And I'm pretty sure I know who created this math competition. And I think I've got some data on the other people competing. So, first things first, the creator of this competition: I'm putting my money on a guy named Kyle Wellman. He owns a private equity firm. I think I've met him a couple of times at charity events, and he's a grade-A douchebag, just a heads up."

"Good to know. How do you know he created this?"

"So, most people scan QR codes without knowing how much information can be tracked through them. The dates and times of scans, of course, but also the locations where a code was scanned. A few other things can be tracked as well, but for our purposes, those are the ones we want. I hacked into the analytics software linked to the code in question and found all their data. I then sorted it by date to find the earliest scan of this code in particular. What's the first thing anybody does when they're trying something new?"

"They test it," I replied straight away.

"Exactly. So I figured the first scan would tell us at the very least what company was behind the code, and it did. I got exact GPS coordinates leading back to Kyle's company, Bull Life Equity."

I rolled my eyes. "You didn't have to tell us he was a douchebag. You just had to tell us that was what he named his company, and we could have figured it out from there."

Fiona chuckled. "No kidding. Anyway, I knew it was someone at Bull Life, and I checked the second scan. It was from Kyle's home. He's the one running this competition, no doubt about it."

"Great. I guess we know who we're going to go visit. Listen, Fiona, since you finished that so quickly, do you mind finding any social media DMs and data you can for Ellie Jacobs?"

"Sure. I'll see what I can find. Do you have her physical phone?"

Ophelia gave a wry smile. "What do you think?"

"I love a challenge. Okay, I'll let you know what I find."

"Thanks. Poppy and I are going to go talk to Kyle. We'll see what we can find out about that competition and whether or not he's our killer."

Chapter 8

Bull Life Equity's offices weren't far from Ophelia's office building, in the heart of the financial district, so we walked. They were on California Street, on the 28th floor of an office building whose glass windows were broken up by the large concrete columns that rose skyward from the ground floor. Architecturally, the building had a bit of a brutalist '70s look to it, but as soon as we stepped inside, we found ourselves in a modern, bright, renovated interior and headed straight to the elevators.

The doors opened onto an office that took up the entire floor. Pale grey tile and beige walls were brightened by enormous works of art hanging on the wall and colorful chairs that dotted the waiting area. The style of one of the paintings looked familiar. In front of us was a very fancy, large metal desk etched with an abstract design, and behind it sat a young blond woman, dressed professionally, her hair tied back, speaking into a headset. She motioned for us to wait a second, finished her call, then turned her attention toward us.

"Welcome to Bull Life Equity. Do you have an appointment?"

"We don't, but we need to speak with Kyle Wellman as soon as possible."

The woman didn't so much as blink as she replied, "I'm sorry, but Mr. Wellman is very busy and unable to take unscheduled visits at the moment. What is this concerning?"

"Murder."

At this, the woman's stony façade fractured just a sliver as her lips opened almost imperceptibly. "Murder?"

"Yes, murder."

"Well, I'm afraid you're in the wrong place entirely. There's no way Mr. Wellman would be involved in anything like that. You're not with the police, are you?"

"We're not. We're better."

"I can't allow you to speak with Mr. Wellman without a lawyer, I'm afraid."

"All right, that's fine. In that case, we will come back with the police. I'd be more than happy to show them around this reception area. For example, I think they would really enjoy this piece of art, don't you?" Ophelia said, motioning to the large canvas I'd noticed on the way in.

Read Between the Lies

"Sure?" the woman replied, confusion written all over her features. "It's a nice painting."

"It is, isn't it?" Ophelia said, eyeing it casually. "I must say, though, it wouldn't really be appreciated right off the bat. Most police officers I know will see it as a handful of random shapes that have no meaning. They wouldn't think twice about it. But me, I recognize a Kandinsky when I see one. And this? This is an original."

"Mr. Wellman is a rich man."

"So he is. So rich that he can have in his possession a fifty-million-dollar painting. Normally, that wouldn't be a problem. But this painting was stolen from a small museum in Portugal seventeen years ago."

At this, the receptionist inhaled sharply. "What? No, there's no way."

"I suggest you get Mr. Wellman on the phone right now, tell him what I've just told you, and see if he still wants me to bring the police and a warrant with me."

I turned back to look at the painting in awe while the receptionist whispered into her headset. Fifty million dollars? Art was wild. I knew Wassily Kandinsky had been one of the most prominent members of the Bauhaus movement, but fifty million was still a lot of money for a single canvas. A moment later, the receptionist rose, and my thoughts about the cost of modern art flew to the back of my mind. "Will you follow me, please?"

The receptionist led us through frosted glass doors to a large open office lined with white desks. Every ten feet or so sat another person's workstation. Everybody had three, sometimes four monitors. One even had five. The place buzzed with excitement; the thirty or so people on the floor all had either a phone to their ear, their fingers clacking away on their keyboards, or both.

We walked past the chaos to a set of offices at the back of the room. The receptionist knocked twice on a thick wooden door then opened it, allowing us in.

Kyle Wellman's office had a stunning view over San Francisco. Directly behind him, Coit Tower was perched on its grassy hill, a green oasis in the middle of the city. Behind it, Alcatraz sat in the bay, so close and yet so far for the prisoners who spent years there.

The office itself was equally stunning. To begin with, it was the size of my entire apartment. The floor here was a plush beige. An L-shaped mahogany desk acted as the centerpiece of the room, but to the left was a smaller, round table surrounded by four chairs for an intimate meeting. I couldn't help but notice there was no sign of an actual personality in here. The most interesting decoration was the snake plant in the corner of the room.

But then I supposed that meant there also

weren't any stolen masterpieces, either, so that was a plus.

Kyle Wellman sat behind the main desk. The corner of the L held four monitors, but their positioning allowed him to look at anyone entering head-on. He didn't bother standing when we entered, so I couldn't make out his height, but he was of medium build, wearing a perfectly tailored navy suit. His pale face was clean-shaven, and his hair was brushed and gelled back, like he was trying to hide the fact that he was starting to go bald despite obviously not being a day over thirty-five.

He was also scowling at us like Ophelia had just stolen his lunch money.

As soon as the receptionist closed the door behind us, Kyle spoke. "I don't like being threatened."

"I don't like thieves."

"I didn't steal that painting."

"Right, you just happened to buy a Kandinsky from a guy selling it out the back of a truck."

"It's a fake," Kyle said with a casual shrug.

"We both know it's not."

"Well, that's news to me," Kyle said, his tone of voice and expression betraying the total lie, arrogance coating his words. This was a guy who was used to getting what he wanted without any problems. Fiona was right. He was a total and complete douchebag. I was surprised he wasn't wearing a puka shell necklace. "I was told it was a fake, and I don't believe otherwise."

"Okay," Ophelia said, taking a seat in the chair across from Kyle. I slipped into the one next to her. "How about this: you tell me everything I need to know about this math competition you're running, and I won't go to Interpol and tell them a painting they've been looking for is hanging on the wall of an office in San Francisco. After all, if it really is a fake, you won't mind me giving them a heads up. I have a friend who works in their art theft division. His name is Jean-Paul. I'm quite certain he'd be willing to authenticate this painting for you, if you wish."

"I'm sure we don't want to bother your friend over a fake painting," Kyle said with a forced smile. "I'll take you up on this offer. What competition are you talking about?"

Ophelia turned the phone toward him and showed Kyle the poster.

"Oh, that. I like to consider it a job interview."

"So you admit you're the one running it."

"Sure am. And a couple of the contestants are getting close to the end too. I'm giving it another week or so, and I'm going to have my newest employees. I'll probably offer jobs to a few of these kids taking part."

"Why don't you run us through it? Why do this sort of game? Why not interview people normally?"

Kyle leaned back in his chair, grinning. "Math is, in my opinion, the single most important disci-

Read Between the Lies

pline in the history of the world. As people, without it, we have nothing. Most of the world, they don't understand the potential of using math. They think they're just numbers, stuff you add and subtract. But with the right person, math can make you millions. This competition is to find out who has the math skills, the creative mind, and also the personality to make it in this place. I started Bull Life Equity myself, right out of college. I had a bit of seed money from my father's company, but I ballooned it into this place you see now. I did that with math, but it's not just the numbers. It's my personality. I like a challenge, and I love to win. There's nothing in the world that makes me happier than beating somebody else at their own game, and I'm very good at it."

"I suppose I should warn you, we have that in common," Ophelia said, her eyes sparkling.

"The thing is, I know what kind of person I want here," Kyle continued, ignoring Ophelia's warning. "I know who has to work for me and the kind of personality they have to have. They need to be competitive. I don't hire just anybody. My standards are high, and if you don't want to be the best, there's no place for you here. That's why the competition works as a job interview. I get to watch some of the brightest minds in the world compete for a job. I get to see who has what it takes. Who's competitive enough to want it and who has the math skills behind it to back it up and make me hundreds of millions of dollars. That's why I do it as a competition, because it shows so much more insight into a person than any job interview ever could."

"Until it turns out one of those people is a murderer," Ophelia said.

"What murder?"

"Yesterday, just a couple of blocks from here."

"Right, I saw the commotion in the afternoon when I left."

"The young woman who was murdered was one of the competitors in your job interview, as you put it."

Kyle's face paled slightly, and for the first time, he actually did look a bit off-kilter. "What?"

"You heard me."

"Which one was it?"

"Ellie Jacobs. She was working with Oliver Dorchester, the chess Grandmaster."

"I *knew* that moron wasn't doing it by himself," Kyle said, slapping his hand on his thigh in triumph. "I knew it. I just couldn't prove it."

"That's certainly not the reaction I'd expect from someone who found out a young woman was just murdered," I said, raising my eyebrows.

"Look, people get killed all the time. It happens. It's sad for her, sad for her family. Whatever. I didn't know her, and it affects me if someone was cheating in that game. I was surprised when I saw Dorchester show up for a clue. I know his background is in math, but he's a chess guy full-time, now. What was he doing? And how was he winning? I couldn't figure it out. He's not a top-tier math guy. There are hundreds of people in this town who are better at it than he is. So how was he winning my contest? Working with someone else explains it. But now she's dead? That's too bad. If I'd have known, I would have offered her a job."

"She wouldn't have taken it. There's a reason she was working behind the scenes," I said.

"Oh, she would have. The salary I was going to offer alone would have enticed her, no matter where else she was working."

"People make decisions based on more than that," I said. "In Ellie's case, who she was working with was more important."

"She would have been reporting directly to me."

My voice was frosty when I said, "Exactly."

Kyle scowled at me.

"Where were you, yesterday, between the hours of one and two o'clock?" Ophelia asked.

"Here. In my office. On a video conference call. There are twelve people who can confirm that for you, if you think I'm a killer. I'm not. If this chick was the one giving Dorchester the answers, I wanted her for my team. I wouldn't have killed her."

"What would have happened if Dorchester won?" Ophelia asked. "Would you have given him the job offer?"

Kyle shrugged. "I guess so. A deal's a deal. And

who knows? Maybe he's not as bad at math as I thought he was. I looked into him, but people change. He got way better at chess this year, didn't he? Maybe he did the same with math. I didn't really believe it, but you never know."

"Did you know him before?" I asked. "It sounds like you know a lot about him."

"I did some deep dives into everyone that's looking like they might win this competition."

"Then you wouldn't mind giving us those names," Ophelia said.

"What if I do mind?"

"Do you know the penalty for possession of stolen property?"

Kyle glared at Ophelia then reached over to his mouse. He worked at the computer for a minute, and the printer behind him eventually whirred to life. Grabbing the paper that came out the other end, he thrust it at her.

"Here. This is everyone I was looking at."

"How did you know who was competing?" I asked.

"I had secret cameras installed at most of the clue locations, especially the early ones. I wanted to see who was playing. After all, this *is* a job interview. That's the other reason I was suspicious of Dorchester. Every time he showed up to a clue that I had wired, he looked like a freaking hermit who'd just crawled out of his hole for the first time in

Read Between the Lies

twenty years. Always looking around, as if someone was after him. It was weird."

"He didn't want it revealed that he was competing," Ophelia said. "He was doing this in a rather misguided attempt to fix his chess reputation and show that he knew what he was doing."

"By trying out for a job with me? Idiot. Win a game against that Austrian lady that beat him a few months back. That's what he needs to do to get his reputation back in order. And fix up that cheating scandal, whatever it takes."

"You will find no disagreement from me on that point," Ophelia said, scanning the list. "So, if you didn't murder Ellie, does anyone on this list stick out to you as someone who might have done it? Someone who could have figured out she was involved and decided to get rid of the competition? After all, you did say that Dorchester was winning."

"He was, and it was a narrow margin. Mia Park —you'll see her there—was right behind him."

"We spoke to her already."

"Then you don't think she's your killer? Look, I'll be honest, no one on this list stands out to me as someone walking down the street wearing a Michael Myers mask."

"Murderers rarely do, in my experience," Ophelia said. "There is a million-dollar prize for the winner, after all."

"Yeah. I get that. And the job, which is arguably

even more valuable than that. The money is just extra incentive to be the best."

"As you say, incentive."

"You have the list. Feel free to go through it. No one stuck out to me as a killer, and I'm a pretty good judge of people, but I haven't actually met any of these ones yet."

"Did you have a camera at *every* stop?" I asked.

"No. There's a few where it wouldn't work. The one Dorchester didn't get to, one of the batteries in the Presidio—I didn't have eyes on that."

"What about the one before it?" Ophelia asked.

"No. I was mainly focused on the first few and the last few. Those are the middle ones."

"All right, thank you," Ophelia said, standing. "I think that's all we need for now."

"We have a deal, right? You're not going to tell anyone about my fake painting?"

"We do. Thank you for the help."

"I would have convinced her to work for me, you know. The dead chick. If I'd found out who she was, I'd have gotten her on board."

"Sure you would, bud," I said as patronizingly as I could as we left. On our way back toward the elevators, my eyes were drawn back to the Kandinsky on the wall.

When we reached the ground floor of the building and were finally outside, I turned to Ophelia. "Well, I didn't expect to be in the presence of a stolen fifty-million-dollar painting today."

"No," she said, her lips curling upward into an amused smile. "It was rather an interesting turn of events, wasn't it?"

"Why hang something like that right on the wall outside, though? You were right. It was the real thing. That much was obvious from his reaction."

"Arrogance. Someone like Kyle Wellman doesn't believe that he'll ever be caught. He puts that painting up as a middle finger to everybody who passes by that office, and I am quite certain that he enjoys his own little joke at everyone's expense."

"It's a risk, but then someone like Kyle Wellman lives his whole life taking risks."

"Indeed. Did you notice how he mentioned that he got his start?"

I grinned. "Yeah. A self-made man, apart from the small investment his father made to allow him to start the business."

"People like that need to believe they are entirely self-made, as admitting they were given an enormous launch up into space goes against the idea they have of themselves and that they need to promote: that there's something special about them."

"Are you going to tell Interpol about the painting?" I asked.

"I'm not sure yet."

"You aren't going to keep your word?"

"I told him I wouldn't, but I also have no problem lying to someone who knowingly purchased a stolen masterpiece. Especially one that was stolen from where the public could view it, to be hung as a metaphor for the new owner's virility in the lobby of a private equity fund. I certainly would like the painting to be returned to its rightful place in a museum. We will see. I have some work to do."

My phone began to ring, and when I saw it was Leon Books calling me, my heart leapt up into my throat.

"Hello?"

"Hi, Poppy. This is Danielle at Leon Books. Given the tragedy that occurred yesterday, you've been assigned a new editor, Francesca Romani. She wants to meet with you today, at one o'clock, at the office."

"Sure, I'll be there."

"Thanks, Poppy."

I said goodbye to Danielle and ended the call, checking the time on my phone as I did so. It was just after twelve-thirty.

"I have to go," I said to Ophelia. "Meeting with the new editor."

"That's rather quick. Good luck!"

"Thanks!"

I turned on my heel and headed in the opposite direction. I should have just enough time to head home, grab my laptop with all of my files on it, and get back to the Leon Books headquarters in time for my meeting with Francesca.

Chapter 9

AT EXACTLY TWO MINUTES PAST ONE, I WAS IN THE lobby at Leon Books.

Given the short time between the phone call and the meeting, I hadn't really had time to process the fact that I'd already been assigned a new editor. That seemed fast, but then, what did I know about the publishing world? Maybe this was normal.

And since I was having a meeting here, maybe I could learn some more about Ellie. This was a good opportunity to see if I could uncover anyone at work who might have wanted her dead.

Besides, I was excited to meet Francesca. Ellie and I had hit it off basically straight away, and I was hoping things would be the same with my new editor.

Leon Books was located on the fourth floor of another skyscraper in the financial district. I stepped out of the elevator and followed the signs down the hall. When I opened the door, I found myself in a reception area. It was professional but with a large bookshelf that took up the entire right-hand wall. On the others were framed covers of some of the company's bestsellers, complete with autographs from the authors.

Danielle was the receptionist working at the desk directly in front of me, according to her name tag. In her thirties, with her black hair in a pixie cut, everything about her was small and dainty. She was efficient, friendly, and talkative, which was a plus for me.

"I'll let Francesca know you're here," she said with a smile when I arrived. She tapped at the computer for a minute then turned to me. "How are you holding up? I heard you were there with Ellie when… it happened."

I nodded. "It was awful. I feel so bad for her. And for her family. How are things here?"

"Dire. Most of the team that worked with her directly was given the day off today, obviously," Danielle said, lowering her voice. "Her desk has become a sort of shrine, and we've got grief coun- sellors available for anyone who needs it. The whole editing team is broken up about this. Francesca is the only one who came in to work today."

"I just can't imagine who would have done this to Ellie," I said. "Like, surely she's not the type of person who would have had enemies."

"No. Everyone here loved her. She didn't have

problems with anybody. It had to be random, right? Someone with mental health issues or something, who just happened to take it out on her. And that's what makes it so sad, is that it's probably the sort of thing that could have been avoided."

"You think?"

"Well, that's what the police believe, anyway. They were here this morning, they spoke to a few people, including me. They didn't come right out and say it, but the impression I got is that they're looking for a random attacker."

I couldn't say they were one hundred percent wrong, but if they were, that meant it was even more important for Ophelia and me to find the real killer.

"Okay, but what if they're wrong? Could it have been someone in her life?"

"Not a chance. She didn't have any problems. Not that I know of, anyway. I guess you never really know a person, though, do you?"

"Was she in a relationship? I feel awful for her partner if she was."

"I don't think so, but also, Ellie wasn't the type of person to talk about that a lot while she was at the office. She kept to herself a lot. And she really liked math. I'd see her doing all sorts of weird calculations at her desk sometimes. I asked her about it once. She said it helped her clear her mind, that it was relaxing for her. Me? I always thought math was the most stressful thing on the planet. But she obviously liked it. Oh, Francesca just messaged me. You're welcome to go through. Do you know the way?"

I shook my head. "No."

"Oh, okay. I'll take you."

Danielle stood and led me through a frosted glass door into the main floor of the office. The layout was simple, with a modern cubicle setup. Black frames and glass tops made the office look large and more inviting, while still offering some privacy to everyone working. To the left was a set of cubicles where Ellie had obviously worked; most of the desks on that side of the room were empty today. I spotted her desk immediately: not only was the computer missing, but it was covered in flowers, not unlike the shrine on the street only a few blocks from here, where she had been murdered.

Danielle led me past her desk to another, where a woman tapped away at her computer.

"This is Francesca," Danielle said, and the woman turned to meet me. She was in her late forties, maybe early fifties. The dour expression on her face made her age hard to tell. Her dark, curly hair reached her shoulders, and she was dressed in a pastel purple blouse and black pants. A plain gold chain hung around her neck. The bright fuchsia shade of lipstick on her lips didn't really suit her, and she pursed them as she looked at me.

"Poppy Perkins? Well, at least your name is

suited to publishing. People will remember a name like that. Sit."

She motioned to a chair next to her, and I sat down, reaching into my purse to grab my laptop. Danielle flashed me a reassuring smile then headed back to the front reception.

"Now, the first thing you should know is that I don't appreciate being made to wait. I had this appointment set for one o'clock, and it's now nine minutes past."

"I was here just after; you're the one who took five minutes after Danielle told you about my arrival," I pointed out.

"Because if you're not going to respect my time, I'm not going to respect yours."

Okay, well, that was kind of petty. I could see where she was coming from; I normally wasn't the kind of person who showed up late to things, but really? I was two minutes late after she'd given me a thirty-minute notice about this meeting.

I took a deep breath. One of Francesca's colleagues had been murdered just yesterday. She was probably having a bad day, and I didn't want to get off on the wrong foot with someone I was going to be working closely with for the foreseeable future. Especially on my first book deal.

"I'm really sorry. I'll make sure to be on time next time," I said, plastering my best customer-service smile on my face.

"You'd better. Now, I was just assigned this book

yesterday, and I don't know anything about it, because it wasn't supposed to be mine."

"I'm sorry about Ellie."

"I barely knew her. Where are you on this book?"

All right, well, I'd never been accused of being an overly sensitive person before, but Francesca was *cold.*

"Um, I've only just started writing it. Angela sold the contract on the first three chapters. I've written another five in the past week, but they're still in the first-draft stage."

"Good. Let me see what you have so far."

I pulled out my laptop, and opened it, pulling up the file. Francesca took the computer from me, and her eyes skimmed the screen. Her lips pursed as she read.

"Is this it?" she asked when she was finished, closing the lid with a little bit more force than I thought was really necessary and handing the laptop back to me.

"Yes," I replied, trying to ignore the sinking feeling of my heart plunging toward the ground. "I've been busy this past week. I solved a murder, and I got stabbed. I'll get the book done."

"Here's the thing," Francesca said, leaning closer toward me. "I've seen a million authors like you come through these doors and leave again. You think you've hit the jackpot. You had an idea, you've written some of it down, and you sold it based on spec instead of having a finished manuscript. Now, in a way, that makes my job easier, because let me tell you something here, Poppy: every single author that gets their first book deal thinks they're the next Ernest Hemingway. Every single one of them. But let me ask you: how many books have you written?"

"Zero," I admitted. "But I have a master's degree in creative writing. I've done a lot of assignments."

"Do you know what that sounds like to me? That sounds like someone coming up to me and telling me they've never even stepped on a plane before, but they're ready to fly a fighter jet because they did some time in the simulator. Let me do you a favor: forget that you ever did that degree. Everything about it. From now on, it's useless. You know what *will* help you become a better writer? Writing. Every second of every day. Thinking about stories. Living your stories. *Breathing* your stories. And then writing them down. I don't know why publishing seems to be the exception to this rule that to do something well, you have to do it a lot. People are convinced that they can sit down and write a masterpiece on their first go-around. And guess what? They can't. What you've given me right now is a steaming turd that's been set on fire."

My mouth turned into an O. This wasn't what I'd expected at all from my first meeting with my new editor. She'd literally just called the five chapters of my blood, sweat, and tears a steaming turd that had been set on fire?

And she wasn't finished. "That's why I'm here. I've got twenty-five years of experience in this job. My role is to take this book—if you can even call it that at this point—and turn it into something that people will not only want to read but might actually enjoy. That's not what this is right now. Right now, this is shit."

I desperately wanted to say something. Defend myself. Defend my book, which I'd worked hard on. I wasn't a terrible writer. I knew that. Maybe I hadn't written twenty novels before in my life, but this had been my dream. I studied craft. I studied characters. I had a freaking master's degree, for crying out loud. Francesca might think it was just a piece of paper, but it was a piece of paper that I had poured my entire soul into. It was worth more than just a cursory mention as a useless waste of time.

But I also didn't want to burn this new bridge right away. So, for once in my life, I kept my mouth shut. Mostly.

"Now, the fact that you've actually got something here is already a start. But do you know what the number-one problem with new authors is?"

"Their manuscripts are shit?" I offered, a touch of dryness in my voice despite the fact that I was trying not to be antagonistic.

"No. That's *a* problem, but it's not *the* problem. I

can fix that one. What I can't fix is a lazy author. This is your first book contract, right?"

I nodded, not trusting myself to speak.

"Then let me guess what you think your life is going to be like from here: you're going to spend your days in coffee shops. Maybe on a patio. You'll have your laptop out, and you'll people-watch, while telling yourself that you're doing research for your next book. You'll drink coffee, and you'll have meetings with friends. You'll have a pretty little notebook out, something cute, maybe with some gold lettering on the front. You're building up your characters' stories, after all. You'll spend the day there, as you let the story percolate in your mind. Do you notice anything missing?"

"The actual writing part," I said wryly.

"Exactly. That's what most new authors miss. They think the hard work is over. They got the book deal. It's done. They've worked for this for years, and now that they've signed that contract, the hard work is done. Well, let me rid you of that idea right now. The hard work is not done. The hard work hasn't even begun. You have to write the damn thing, and that's where so many people fall down. Do you know how many people say they want to write a book, that they definitely have a novel in them?"

I opened my mouth to respond, but Francesca kept going without skipping a beat; obviously, I wasn't meant to actually answer. "All of them. If I go down onto the street and ask a hundred people if they think they could write a book, they would all tell me yes. That they have an idea for that great novel. And do you know how many of them are going to actually write it? None of them. Because nobody understands just how hard it really is to do until they sit down and try to do it. And I know you're one of them."

"I've got five chapters there already," I argued.

"Oooh, five chapters, I'm so impressed," Francesca said, rolling her eyes.

"Is there a bathroom around here?" I asked quickly. I needed a moment to compose myself. This wasn't what I'd expected at all, and I needed to come up with a game plan.

"Through those doors over there," Francesca said, motioning with her head. "Down the hall."

"Thanks. I'll be right back."

I resisted the urge to sprint toward the door, collapse into a cubicle in a heaping pile, and sob away. I walked calmly over to the door, pushed through, and found myself in a hallway. I leaned against the wall and took a few deep breaths. I was upset, sure. Francesca had just told me my book was awful. That hurt, *especially* since it came from the person who was supposed to help make it better. Work with me to transform it into the best book it could possibly be.

But more than that, I was angry. How dare she? I wasn't a bad writer. Sure, I'd never written a full novel before, but I wrote all the time. And not just for assignments. I read books to help improve my writing. I spent my whole life watching people, seeing how they acted. I lived and breathed this art. It was what I was meant to do. It wasn't just a job for me. This was going to be a way of life. And Francesca had just dismissed me, lumped me in with everyone else without even giving me a chance.

How dare she judge me like this when she'd barely given me a chance to speak two words? And how could I react when I didn't want to ruin this professional relationship before it even started?

The door leading to the hallway swung open suddenly, and I turned, standing quickly and trying not to look like I was in the middle of a miniature meltdown in the middle of this office.

I'd seen the man who walked in on the other side of the room when Danielle had led me to Francesca's desk. He was tall and very slim. His platinum blond hair was gelled to fly out in all directions, and a streak of it was dyed neon pink, which matched his nails.

"So, you're Francesca's latest victim, huh?" he asked me, a wry smile on his face. "I can always tell when they're bringing in new meat."

"That's me," I said, forcing a smile and trying to be cheery about it. "I wasn't expecting this, to be honest."

"No one ever does. Look, let me give you a piece of advice: talk back to her."

"Really? She doesn't seem like she'd enjoy it."

"I know, but that's the secret. She'll respect you that way. If you lie there like a doormat and let her walk over you, she will, and she'll crush you underneath her. I've seen it happen too often. You want to fight her. Argue with her. Fight for your characters. Fight for your books. Fight for what you want."

"And that will make her nicer?"

The man cackled out a laugh. "Oh God, no. Francesca will be a grade-A bitch to you until the day she dies, no matter what. But she'll respect you. And that will make it a little bit easier."

I offered the man a smile. "Thanks. I appreciate the advice."

"Of course, honey. Look, she's hard to handle, but Francesca is the best editor in this place. It doesn't seem like it right now, but you're lucky. She'll make sure your book is as good as it possibly can be."

"Good to know. I was assigned to Ellie before."

The man shook his head sadly. "Poor her. I still can't believe what happened. I didn't really know her; I work in graphic design. But when we did work together, she was nice. I liked her."

"Yeah."

"I hope they find the person who did that to her. All right, I have to go. I have a meeting. But you looked like you were getting your ass kicked out there, and I wanted to give you a bit of a hand."

Read Between the Lies

"Thanks," I said again. The man grinned and winked at me then headed back out.

I went into the bathroom, splashed a bit of water on my face, then steeled myself and headed back out to speak to Francesca again.

When I sat back down, she turned to me. "So, if you've stopped crying, are you going to listen to me? You need to actually write this book. That means sitting down and getting the words on the page."

"Of those five chapters, I wrote two of them in a hospital bed. After getting stabbed," I replied. I motioned to my arm, which was still in its sling. "See this? It's not just for decoration. Someone stabbed me in the shoulder. And with one hand, I still managed to write two chapters, while lying in the hospital. So you can talk about how you think I'm not going to write this book, but you're wasting your breath, and my time. It's going to get done. I want this more than anything in the world. I don't treat this like a job. I don't even treat it like a career. This is my *life*. And I'm not going to be a passenger in my life."

I might have been imagining things, but I could have sworn the corners of Francesca's mouth curled upward into a shadow of a smile for a split second before she replaced it with her familiar scowl.

"Good. You'd better. Because if there's one thing I can't stand, it's the authors who don't meet their deadlines. I want the first draft finished four months from now, because it's going to take a lot of work."

"Why?" I asked. "It's one thing to tell me the book is a steaming turd, as you put it, but that's not going to help me make the book better. What do you hate about it?"

"The characters. Your main character—she's too type A."

"She's supposed to be type A. That's her whole thing. She graduated top of her class from Johns Hopkins."

"That's a problem. She's not relatable. She's too successful."

"She's relatable, because she's flawed, and she has problems. Being successful doesn't make her unrelatable. Being perfect would. And Amanda is far from perfect. She works hard to get what she wants. I don't think making her successful, or making her ambitious, makes her unrelatable. If anything, I think it makes her *more* relatable. We all have ambition. We all work hard to get what we want. Amanda is just unapologetic about it, in a way I think most of us wish we could be."

I paused, and Francesca was silent for a moment, which in a way was even more terrifying than when she was going on about how much I was going to fail.

"Name another main character on TV who's so unapologetically ambitious."

"Christina Yang, on *Grey's Anatomy*. Also a doctor."

"Not the main character."

"All right, *Scandal*, then. Olivia Pope is one of the most powerful people in Washington. She knows it. Media is changing. Women are the main characters in their lives and stories now, rather than side pieces who exist only to further the plots of men. Amanda is one of those. She's going to resonate with women, because women want to be her, and women understand the struggles she's faced, and they want her to overcome her flaws. They *want* to cheer for her. They've always wanted that. We just haven't gotten it all that often until now."

"This opening doesn't work," Francesca replied. Obviously, this conversation about Amanda as a main character was over. Did that mean I'd won the debate? Good, because I wasn't about to change Amanda into a more apologetic version of herself.

"What don't you like about it?"

"You're not building the world at all. You're throwing people right into the action."

"Yes, that's done on purpose. Have you ever read a book where the first twenty pages are the author explaining the backstory to every single character? Of course. We all have. And they suck. You don't usually get to the end of it because you're already bored, and you've put the book down. I have opened this right in the middle of an action scene. Amanda is saving someone's life in the operating room after they were in a car accident. It's all about how good she is at her job. It shows that she's a hard worker, that she knows what she's doing, and that she is respected in her workplace."

This conversation continued for a while. A couple of hours, even. Eventually, Francesca leaned back in her chair.

"Okay. Let's meet again when you have more of this book done. We need to sort out deadlines too. I want your first draft within four months. It's going to require so many rewrites. We'll have to go over every sentence. Every single word in a book matters."

I met her gaze with a steely one of my own. "That's fine with me." I wasn't about to let Francesca think I was a pushover and that I was afraid of hard work.

"I don't give praise out often, but this book might not end up being quite as horrible as I thought when I first read it."

Francesca gave praise out like my mother.

"It will be ready in time."

"Good."

Realizing this was my cue, I stood up and got ready to leave. "Do we make another appointment, then?"

"Here's my card. Call me when you're close to finishing your first draft," Francesca said. "Some editors like to work chapter-by-chapter but not me. I want to see the full, finished work. And don't disappoint me. Do not fall into the trap of thinking that just because you've got a book contract, the hard work is done. It isn't. The hardest part of this job hasn't even started yet. Don't be another failure that I have to chase, because that is the worst part of my job, and I will not do it."

"Understood," I said coldly.

I packed my laptop up into my bag and headed toward the exit.

When I left the main floor and walked into the reception area, I saw Juliette. My former best friend. I had to admit, she looked good. Her blond hair flowed down her back, and she was talking with Danielle and another woman next to her that I recognized. This was Audrey Delibes, one of the biggest authors in the world. She had won the Agatha Award last year for the best new mystery release. She was constantly featured in magazines and on TV, and she could weave a whodunnit like nobody else.

Juliette had just said something that made Audrey laugh. Audrey was on the shorter side, maybe five foot two, with gorgeous caramel waves that brushed her shoulders. She looked exactly like she did in her author photo, and if it weren't for the presence of my former best friend, I totally would have fangirled and asked for an autograph.

At the sound of the door opening, however, Juliette turned, and when her eyes landed on me, they narrowed.

"Poppy. What are you doing here?"

"Haven't you heard?" Danielle chimed in from behind the desk. "Poppy Perkins is our latest signing. I didn't realize the two of you knew each other."

"We used to," I replied coolly.

"Audrey, this is Poppy," Juliette said, a smirk on her face. "Her mom is a famous lawyer, and I guess finally got her a contract here. For now. I imagine it's only one book, right?"

"It is," I replied with a smile that didn't reach my eyes. I knew Juliette was about to brag, but I wasn't going to stoop down to her level. Not in public, anyway. "I'm very excited to be working with Leon Books."

"Oh, this is *that* Poppy," Audrey said, looking at me like I was a steaming turd on the sidewalk, just like Francesca thought my book was.

"It is. I don't recommend introducing yourself, Audrey. You won't be seeing her a whole lot. It's nice that the company took a chance on her, but it's not going to amount to anything."

"Given as my advance per book is bigger—a lot bigger—that really doesn't say much about what they think about you," I replied, my mouth curling into a smirk. Whoops. So much for not being petty in front of everyone else.

"Come on, Audrey," Juliette snapped. "We have better things to do than to stand here and talk to *her*."

Juliette glared at me, and I held her stare as she

walked past, with Audrey behind her, not even offering me a second glance.

I shouldn't have let it bother me, but it did. Juliette already knew people here. She had friends. I had Francesca.

"I'm guessing there's a history there?" Danielle said from behind the desk.

I sighed. "Yeah. Sorry. Juliette brings out the worst in me." I didn't want to go around telling everyone what Juliette had done. They probably wouldn't believe me anyway. I was going to have to let my own success do the talking for me.

"Don't worry about it. How was your meeting with Francesca?"

"She's not Ellie, that's for sure," I replied with a tight smile.

"You're not wrong."

"It went well, though. I think. About as well as it could have."

"Glad to hear it. It was nice meeting you, Poppy. I'm sure I'll see you around."

"Yeah."

I said goodbye to Danielle and headed out into the street. I couldn't help but feel like someone had replaced my heart with a brick.

Chapter 10

I ALWAYS THOUGHT THE SCARIEST PART ABOUT living out my dreams would have been getting started. Gathering the courage to try, knowing that there was a chance I could fail. After all, failing at something you don't care about is fine. Whatever. It happens all the time. When I was in the second grade, Mom thought I should learn to play a musical instrument, beyond the recorder that my teacher taught us to use during music class. And I say "taught" in the loosest sense of the word.

The CIA should have dropped a few Guantanamo inmates into that music class; they would have gotten all the intel they could have dreamed of within minutes, with thirty seven-year-olds failing at playing "Hot Cross Buns" on recorders.

Anyway, that year, Mom decided it would look good on my law school applications if I also happened to be a virtuoso on another instrument.

While my sister Megan took to the violin immediately, I did not. Within weeks she was playing Bach, while I both looked and sounded like I was struggling to cut an angry stray cat's nails.

So, when I had to admit I failed, it didn't matter. I hated the violin. It's not like I was heartbroken the day Mom finally admitted that I was never going to be the next Hilary Hahn, and let me quit.

But when it came to something important, failure seemed scary. And that's what made it so hard for people to take the first step. I knew that.

What I hadn't considered is what happens when your dream life turns into a nightmare.

What happens when the life you imagined, the life you thought you were going to live, is nothing like the dream you worked toward your whole life?

This was even more terrifying.

I'd always wanted to be an author. I had signed my book deal. But now my editor was a monster who seemed to want to chew me up and spit me out for breakfast. One of my literary heroes, a woman I looked up to and whose books I adored, thought I was scum, because Juliette had gotten to her first.

Maybe I'd made the wrong decision in signing with Leon Books. I went with because they had a reputation for releasing great books and putting a marketing engine behind their top authors. But I wasn't going to lie—a part of me wanted to show Juliette up at her own publisher.

But she'd had more chances to meet people. Her

first editor hadn't been murdered. She wasn't working with someone who was basically a Balrog incarnate. She had friends here that were other authors, and I didn't. My chances of meeting them were slim too. Juliette had already poisoned that whole well.

I checked my phone to find nothing from Ophelia, so I headed back home, stopping into LLB on the way. Now that it was the afternoon, it was a lot quieter than this morning, and when I saw Laura Belle behind the counter. I smiled. Her big, blond hair had apparently never learned the eighties were over, and today she wore a neon pink blouse with jeans.

"Well, hello there, darlin'," Laura Belle drawled in her southern accent. "What's going on? You're looking lower than a bow-legged caterpillar."

"Is it that obvious?" I asked with a small smile.

"Let me put it this way: don't ever play poker with real stakes."

"Good to know. I'm okay. Just dealing with some stuff. It turns out living out my dream isn't going exactly the way I thought it would."

"That's because your dream isn't a single moment in time."

"What do you mean?"

"It's called living your dream, honey. It's not having your dream. There isn't one single moment that you can pin down as your dream, and that's all of it. With a few exceptions. The players on the

Saints obviously dream of winning the Super Bowl. That's a moment in time. But you? Your dream is to be a successful author. That's more than just a moment in time. That's a life. And like with anything else in life, it'll never be all sunshine and rainbows."

"I guess I've never considered that."

"For Lily and me, opening this place was our dream. We wanted to make a place that members of the LGBT community and residents of Chinatown could call home. We wanted to make a safe space for members of communities that didn't always feel safe. And it wasn't easy, especially at first. Our second month of business, the coffee machine we'd bought broke down, and Lily had to max out all her credit cards so we could buy a new one. Then we had a flood. One of the apartments upstairs had their hot water tank explode, and we were closed for a week while it was all fixed. We were living so close to the bone, there were times where we were fixin' to drop our apartment lease and sleep on the benches at night just to save ourselves some cash. It didn't feel like we were living a dream then."

"No, I imagine not."

"And right now, you're at the beginning of this step in your life. You're walking into your dream, but you've just barely crossed the threshold. Honey, I know you feel like life's passed you by, but you're not even thirty yet. You're starting on the path to

Read Between the Lies

your dream, but you haven't reached that peak yet. And sure, on the way, you're going to get some gorgeous views, but there will be valleys. You just have to hang in there like a hair in a biscuit and keep moving. Because frankly, your only other option is giving up, and isn't that worse?"

"Yeah," I said, feeling the brick in my chest get a bit lighter. "You're right. It's not the end of the world. And my new editor might be a mean person, but someone told me she's one of the best in the business, so in the long term, if I can put up with her, it'll help me overall."

"There you go. See? Always a silver lining somewhere."

"Thanks, Laura Belle."

"Anytime, honey. You know I love you a bushel and a peck. You're a smart cookie. You'll figure it all out."

"What if I made the wrong choice, though?"

"Well, the thing about life is you've almost always got choices, and very few of them are going to kill you. Is this choice going to kill you?"

"I don't think so."

"Then you keep going, you see what happens, and you make the next choice accordingly. As I said, you're living your dream. Present tense. The future, it's gonna keep coming. It's not going to stop for you. You just have to make the best decision you can with the information you have."

I nodded. "That makes sense. Thanks."

"Don't you worry about it. Now, what are you having?"

I placed my order and sat down at my regular table in the corner, pulling out my laptop and opening it. The cursor blinked on the Word document as I stared at it. Francesca's words ran through my head. The manuscript, as it stood, was a steaming turd that she was going to have to turn into a masterpiece.

I hated that that was how she viewed this book. Sure, it wasn't perfect yet. I had no doubts about that. I'd only just started writing it yet, and I hadn't edited a single page. But it was better than a turd, and I was going to prove it.

I began typing away, mashing the keys with a little bit more gusto than I usually did. I was going to show her. And I was going to show Juliette, Audrey, and everyone else at that company who thought I was a loser who had no chance of succeeding, who'd only just gotten a book deal because of who my mom was.

I laughed inwardly at that thought. If only they knew. Juliette knew. That was why she'd said it, of course. She was well aware of how much that would hurt me.

I typed awkwardly with a single hand until my phone pinged next to me. The text was from Nick, the journalist I'd met when I was the prime suspect in Jason Bergman's murder.

Hey, Poppy. Just checking in to see how you're doing. Do you want to grab some dinner or something?

My heart swelled as I read his message. I liked Nick. He was one of the few people that had come to visit me in the hospital. I'd texted him to let him know about the offer from Leon Books, and he'd seemed genuinely excited.

That sounds great, I replied. We organized to meet at seven o'clock at a Japanese place Nick swore was the best in the city, and I sent Ophelia a text.

Any updates?

She replied a minute later. *Tomorrow morning, we will go meet with Anna Mayer. I have a theory, and I would like to see if it pays off. It should be an interesting day.*

If Ophelia said it would be interesting, I was totally in. A boring day for her was more interesting than some of the craziest days of my life.

LBB Café was getting ready to close up for the night, so I headed upstairs, kept writing my book, and tried to keep Francesca's voice out of my head. I wasn't a terrible writer. And I was going to prove it.

A COUPLE OF MINUTES TO SEVEN, I WAS WALKING up to Nippon Curry. Located in a hole-in-the-wall building between an apartment complex on one side and a large bar on the other, the exterior was unassuming, with just a blue sign advertising the business name. However, when I entered, I found myself in the middle of a bustle of activity. There was a counter from which to order, and behind it the kitchen, the sound of oil sizzling away reaching my ears as workers shouted to one another in Japanese.

I looked around; most of the tables were taken, and Nick was sitting at one against the wall. He flashed me a smile and a small wave when he saw me, which I returned before stepping up to the counter to place my order.

Slipping across from him at the table with my drink, I smiled. "Hi. Thanks for the text."

"Of course. I wanted to see how you're doing. How's the shoulder?"

"Getting there. Honestly, probably the least interesting thing about my life right now."

Nick nodded. "A friend of mine showed me some photos that were taken of the crime scene today. I saw you in the background. I'm sorry. Did you know her?"

"She was my editor. We'd just met that day for lunch. We were walking back to the office so she could introduce me to a few people. I didn't know her well, but she was nice."

"I'm sorry."

"Thanks. I'm trying to solve her murder, with Ophelia. I kind of figure it's the least I can do."

"Technically, the least you can do is nothing and let the police solve it."

"True. But I'm not going to do that."

"What are you thinking?"

"Well, it turns out she was a math prodigy, but she left that world. She was working with a chess Grandmaster, though. Oliver Dorchester."

Nick grinned. "Oh, I know that guy. I did a little bit of research into him a few months ago."

"The cheating thing?"

"Exactly."

"What did you find?"

"That's the problem: nothing. The story didn't go anywhere, because for there to be a story, I needed to prove Dorchester was cheating. And as far as I could tell, he wasn't."

"Do you think he was? Like, personally, regardless of the evidence?"

"I'm not sure," Nick replied slowly. "My instinct was to say yes. After all, these rumors don't come from nowhere. There have been accusations in the past, although Dorchester always denied them. Every single time. The only thing I found was that Dorchester got caught cheating on a test once in college. I spoke to the professor. It was an elective biology class. Dorchester apologized, accepted the zero mark, and did extra work for the professor to make up for it, so he was allowed to pass the class, and it never showed up on his record. It was only by chance that I found out about it. The professor said Dorchester swore up and down that it wasn't the kind of person he was, and that he just panicked, and that given his actions afterward, the professor believed him."

"See, I hate people who say that after they get caught doing something wrong. It *does* reflect who you are, because your actions *are* a reflection of who you are. If you sit there and *say* your values are those of a vegetarian, but you go out and eat a beef burger every single night, your actions show that vegetarianism isn't one of your values at all."

"I completely agree with you. I do believe people can change their values, but the question is, has Dorchester?"

"In this case, I can confirm that he has not," I said with a wry smile. "It has nothing to do with chess, but he was definitely cheating at another game, along with Ellie."

"No kidding? That's not a huge surprise, I guess. And it goes to show that he is still a cheater at heart. But no, my story went nowhere, because I couldn't find any proof that he was doing anything untoward while playing chess."

"How would it be done, if he had?"

"There are a few ways someone could try to get away with it, according to the people I spoke to. The first is to use a chess engine during the game; basically, a computer that tells you what the right next move is."

"Like the computer that beat Kasparov all those years ago?"

"Exactly. So, in my research, I found that

someone had theorized that it could be possible to set something up inside your shoes, where you would use your toes to tell the computer what moves were just played, and the computer would tell you what to do next."

"In your toes? Wow."

"Yeah. Of course, there were other jokes made as well, about how it could be a butt plug, that sort of thing."

I snorted with laughter.

"But," Nick continued, "in reality, I don't think that was how Dorchester was doing it, if he was cheating. Apparently, security looked in his shoes before his big matches after the news came out."

"Well, the thing is, he's not a bad player on his own," I pointed out. "I mean, he's the third-best player in the world. And he does lose games."

"Right, but it would look even more suspicious if he was unstoppable."

I shook my head. "He wouldn't have lost to Anna Mayer. I don't believe that. We spoke to him about her, and he really dislikes her. I think he would have preferred to lose to a thousand other men rather than have her take over the second-in-the-world spot by beating him. But then, he might not have been cheating every game. He's obviously got skills."

"Exactly. So, the other option is that he was getting someone else to help him. Maybe someone in the crowd. That's harder to pull off, because there is security. People watching. But you never know."

"Someone like the woman helping him cheat at another game," I mused.

"Ellie? You think she was helping him?" Nick asked.

"The more I hear about this, the more likely I think it is. He lied to us about how long he'd known her for too. He told us he ran into her two months ago, but she was in the crowd at his game against Anna Mayer a few months ago. Maybe it was tit-for-tat. She helped him cheat at chess, and he helped her win the money in that math competition from afar. Maybe they weren't actually going to split the money; maybe that money was Ellie's payment for helping Dorchester cheat. A kind of I scratch-your-back-you-scratch-mine kind of situation."

"So do you think he's the killer?"

"I think he's the prime suspect, for sure."

"What would the motive be, though, if she was helping him?"

I shrugged. "Maybe Ellie decided she had enough. Maybe she didn't want to be involved in his cheating anymore. From what I heard, her exit from the math world was abrupt and thorough. She didn't want to go back to it. She might have figured that if Dorchester got caught, she would end up in his spotlight, and that was something she didn't want to do."

"So he killed her?"

I nodded. "I mean, I've certainly heard worse motives."

At that moment, someone called our names. Nick went up to the counter and returned with two steaming plates of thick Japanese curry poured over a generous portion of sticky rice, topped with katsu pork, carrots, and potatoes.

The aroma set my mouth watering, and I immediately unwrapped my set of chopsticks and dug in.

After we'd both made decent headway into our plates, I asked, "How about you? How's your investigation into Klickd going?"

Nick was an investigative reporter with a monthly magazine in San Francisco, one of the most prestigious in the country.

"So far so good. This is going to turn into an exposé for sure. I can't speak about it too much at the moment, but I've been interviewing people at Klickd, and I'm getting more and more to go on. This isn't just rot on the surface of the company. It goes down to the core."

"I'm not entirely surprised," I said with a wry smile.

"I can't say more, but it's going to be explosive when it comes out."

"Good. There's a lot of stuff happening in this town right now that feels like it needs to be exposed."

"There sure does. What happens now, with your book? Since Ellie was your editor?"

"I was assigned a new one. Francesca. And honestly, she gives off nightmare-teacher vibes. You know the type. Nothing is ever good enough for them, and they think punishment and berating are the way to get someone to work hard."

"Ugh. Sorry to hear."

"Eventually, I took a break, and a guy at least took pity on me and told me to stand up to her, that she'd respect me more if I did. And that didn't really make things easier. She was still awful. But at least I didn't have to sit there feeling like I was just taking a whole bunch of abuse for nothing. And I saw Juliette. Basically, the whole thing can be summed up as a disaster. I don't know. I wonder if I made the wrong choice, going with Leon Books."

"You had other offers, right?"

I nodded. "Yup."

"If Juliette didn't exist, and wanting to get back at her didn't factor into your decision making at all, what would you have done? Who would you have signed with?"

I considered Nick's question as I moved a carrot around on my plate with the chopsticks. "You know, I think I still would have signed with Leon Books."

"Did you know Ellie was going to be your editor then?"

"No. They didn't tell me who it would be. And even if I had, it's not as if I have a network of people I could ask, to see what each one would be like."

"So essentially, you still made what would have been the best decision for yourself with the knowledge you had at the time."

"I did," I admitted.

"In that case, you have nothing to regret. You wouldn't have made a different decision at the time, no matter what. You'd still be here. And it's not over. Sure, you dislike your editor. But they're not the one who's writing the book. You are. When's the next time you see her?"

"When I have the book finished. Probably in about four months or so."

"That's not so bad, is it? You have to deal with her then, but for the next four months you're going to be writing your first novel. And who knows? She might get murdered between now and then, too," he added with a grin.

"Oh, don't say that," I said, laughing. "I'm starting to feel like I'm the curse."

"Does that mean I should be watching my back?"

"You never know."

"I hope that if someone does murder me, you'll investigate it and bring them to justice."

"I promise I will. And on that note, if there's anyone out there who wants to kill you, now would probably be a good time to let me know," I replied with a chuckle.

"Luckily, I don't think there is. Not really, anyway. Maybe a few people I wrote articles about."

"This conversation has suddenly gotten a lot more macabre than it should."

"Especially for a third date."

Warmth flooded my cheeks, and I really hoped my face wasn't doing a great impression of a tomato right now. "Don't worry. I only talk about murder with dates I *really* like," I replied. Seriously, why couldn't my mouth try to connect with my brain for even *one second* before speaking? Was that too much to ask for? Especially in front of someone as hot as Nick?

Luckily, he took it in stride and laughed. "I'll take that compliment."

"Good, because it turns out I'm way better at writing than I am at flirting."

"I think you're doing a pretty good job at both right now."

Oh, good, it was round two of tomato-face.

It probably didn't take Albert Einstein to notice I was embarrassed right now, but I was still grateful when Nick changed the subject. I was really, really bad at talking about my feelings.

"So, what's your plan for proving Dorchester is your killer?"

"I'm not sure," I replied. "Ophelia has organized for us to talk to Anna Mayer tomorrow. I don't know if she'll have a lot of evidence to offer up, since it's not like she and Dorchester were besties."

"No. I gathered as much as well."

"It could also have been someone else. But I asked around a bit at the office this afternoon, and no one gave me any signs that there were people who disliked Ellie. I mean, I don't think Francesca, my new editor, liked her very much. She didn't even take the day off that was offered. But I also think Francesca doesn't like most people, and she hasn't murdered everyone she's come into contact with so far."

"If she did, maybe you would be the one who had to look over her shoulder," Nick offered.

"No kidding. I think if anyone can find proof he killed her, though, it will be Ophelia."

"With your help."

"I'm doing what I can."

"Batman never would have gotten anywhere without Robin."

"I think I'm more of a Wonder Woman."

"Okay. Batman and Wonder Woman do make a good team."

I smiled. I might not have liked talking about my feelings very much, but I was certainly starting to feel them for Nick.

Chapter 11

AFTER OUR DATE, NICK AND I WALKED SLOWLY back along the streets of the city to my place.

"So, you live right over your favorite coffee place, huh? That's convenient," Nick said with a grin as we arrived.

"Yeah. I love it. Lily and Laura Belle are the best too. Thanks for dinner."

"Thanks for saying yes," Nick replied. He leaned in and gave me a peck on the cheek, lingering for just a split second. "Do it again sometime?"

"Absolutely," I replied breathlessly.

He paused then spoke. "Have a good night, Poppy."

"You too."

Nick walked back down the street, and I stood frozen in place, my keys hanging from the lanyard in my hand. I didn't know how this worked. Was I supposed to invite him upstairs? Had he been waiting for that? Did I just screw this up by not doing it?

God, why did dating have to be so hard? I was almost thirty. I was supposed to have this nailed down by now. It wasn't supposed to be awkward anymore. And yet here I was, questioning every single decision I'd ever made around him like I was a hormonal fifteen-year-old and had never even kissed a boy before.

I leaned against the outside of the building, closed my eyes, and sighed.

"Poppy?" a voice asked suddenly.

I jumped and opened my eyes to see Steph, Oliver Dorchester's girlfriend, standing about ten feet away.

"Oh, Steph. Hi."

"Sorry to sneak up on you like this. I was actually going to call Ophelia, but I was walking back from a friend's house and saw you. Listen, I have to tell you something."

Steph looked around nervously, as if worried we'd be overheard.

"Sure. Yeah, do you want to come up to my apartment?"

"No. I'll be quick. I wasn't going to say anything. I love Oliver. He's incredible. He's so smart, he's talented, he's everything. But that girl… murder… that's something else. I wasn't sure I wanted to say anything. But if he killed her, he needs to be punished for it."

I stayed silent and let Steph keep talking. She shifted her weight between the balls of her feet; she was obviously nervous and trying to say something. It was an old lawyer's technique: if someone was talking, let them.

"Here's the thing: Oliver was cheating at chess. That woman, Ellie? She was helping him. For months, they'd been working together. They didn't meet by accident two months ago; they got in touch earlier than that. I don't know the details. I didn't want to pry. I thought Oliver was good enough to be the best in the world without cheating, but he's an adult. It's his choice. A week ago, Ellie told him she wasn't going to help him anymore. She said she'd been recognized. Someone contacted her, someone she knew from college. They'd seen her in a crowd, and she couldn't risk it anymore."

"Was Oliver mad?"

"Livid. They had a huge argument. I was upstairs, and I could hear it perfectly. Oliver didn't want her to stop. He said he needed her, but Ellie was adamant. She said she'd built a new life for herself here, one away from all the people in math that she hated, and she just wanted to go back to being a book editor. Oliver told her she'd be sorry and that he wouldn't let her get away with it. Ellie said he wasn't entitled to her, and that was the problem with men. They didn't understand boundaries. Then she left. Oliver was so angry. You know the brown vase in the living room? I had to buy that the other day to replace the one he smashed after she left. It was ugly."

"You obviously think he could have killed her, if you're here."

Steph looked down at the ground. "I don't know. I don't like to think so. After all, he's Oliver. I love him. But at the same time..." she trailed off.

"You wouldn't be here if you didn't have your doubts."

"The day it happened, he was in a mood that day. I chalked it up to him still being annoyed about Ellie. I didn't realize she'd been murdered then. I didn't know until you showed up at our door. But then I thought back, and he was just acting... strange. Even for him. But that doesn't mean he did it. I just want you to find out the truth. If he's innocent, then I'll be the happiest woman in the world. But if he did it, well, I think murder is a crime that should be punished."

"Thank you for telling me."

Steph nodded quickly. "I have to go. Please don't mention this meeting to anyone except Ophelia."

"I won't, I promise. But just quickly—how were they doing it? Do you know?"

"Ellie kept a tiny computer in her pocket. It was disguised, so if she was searched, it would just look like a small notebook. But inside she would get the answers, and she would blink the next move to Oliver. They had a whole code set up, he just barely had to glance in the direction and he would know what to do."

"Why her? Why couldn't, say, you do it?"

"Because everyone in the chess world knows I'm dating Oliver. No one realizes the two of them know each other. They're never seen together. Never in public. No one would think twice about Oliver looking through a crowd of people he didn't know. But if he looked at me regularly in a match, questions would be asked."

"This is a sensitive question, but were they… just playing chess? Or do you think it was more than that?"

"No," Steph said, shaking her head. "No, it was totally platonic, the two of them. I know they used to be close, but I saw them enough. It was all about the chess. The game. The math. I'm not just being a naïve girlfriend either. I knew it was a possibility, and I kept an eye out specifically for that, but no. There was no sign of that. Now, that's enough. I can't talk anymore. I need to get home."

Without another word, Stephanie rushed away from me down the street in a half walk, half jog. She never so much as turned back.

This had obviously been hard for her to admit. I turned, entered the building, and climbed the stairs to my apartment, deep in thought.

Oliver Dorchester had been cheating at more

than just math competitions. The rumors were true; he was cheating his way to the top of the chess world as well. And the person who had been helping him had just quit.

If that wasn't motive for murder, I didn't know what was.

I sent Ophelia a quick text outlining what Steph had just told me, and then I stared at my phone. I knew the phone call I had to make, and I was both excited for and dreading it.

A wave of sadness washed over me, one that I pushed back into the depths of my soul. Most people would have been thrilled to call their parents to let them know they'd gotten a book deal. And yet I knew my mother wouldn't be.

Instead of congratulations and praise, I'd be met with a lecture. I still hadn't told my mother I'd been stabbed, because frankly, I'd rather take a knife to the other shoulder than have to listen to her criticize my actions that led to it happening.

But I was going to make this phone call. I was going to tell her that I'd just been signed. That I'd gotten a book deal. That thing Mom said I'd never be able to do. That was a waste of my time. A waste of my life. I wanted her to know that I was successful despite her. That I was living the life I wanted.

Read Between the Lies

That still didn't mean this was going to be easy.

I was sitting on my mattress on the floor, with my back pressed up against the wall. I leaned my head back. Pressure was starting to build between my eyes, and my mouth was dry. And I hadn't even unlocked my phone yet.

But I was doing this. No question. I pulled out my phone, and before I could lose my nerve, I tapped the button to dial my mom's number. She answered on the second ring.

"Penelope." Her voice was tight, firm. Professional. What was it like having a mom who actually sounded happy to hear from you?

"Hi, Mom. Listen, I have some news."

"I saw they arrested someone for that murder you were suspected of."

"They did. But that's not why I'm calling."

"No?"

"I wanted to let you know I've been offered a book deal. All the contracts are signed, and in about fourteen months, I should be a published author."

The silence on the other end of the line was so thick you could have sliced it with a knife.

"You got a contract, did you?" Mom finally said. I knew that tone. That was her disapproving tone. The tone she used when somebody did something that was good for them but not necessarily good for Mom. I took a deep breath, refusing to be intimidated by it like I was for so much of my childhood.

"That's right. I'm writing a women's fiction

book, I'm getting paid for it, and I've already met my editor. She's great, and I'm really looking forward to working with her."

My mother was like a lion. She stalked, looking for any weakness, and the instant she saw one, she pounced. So, like an antelope with a bit of a limp, I did my best to disguise it and pretend that everything was all good, lest I become her next victim.

"Women's fiction, you say? Well, at least you're not writing one of those smutty novels for Harlequin. If you can even call them that."

"Right, I forgot that anything you don't specifically enjoy is just trash. But don't worry, Mom. This is in a genre that you can tell all your lawyer friends about without being *too* embarrassed of your daughter's life choices."

Mom barked out a laugh on the other end of the line. "Right, because that's what I'm going to tell them, that I have a daughter who's still chasing that childhood dream instead of doing the reasonable thing and going into law. Tell me, Penelope, what is your advance on that book?"

"Eighty thousand."

"Do you know how much money you'd be making in a year if you were a lawyer right now?"

"There is no amount of money in the world that can make up for the hell I'd be living if I was. I don't want to be a lawyer, Mom. This is my dream. This is what I want to do with my life. It's what makes me happy, and I'm finally living it out."

"I didn't realize living in abject poverty for the rest of your life counted as a dream. You were given every opportunity in life, Penelope. You were born into a good family. Your father and I and then I by myself raised you to go into the law. To make something of yourself. To help people, to be financially stable, and to take this family to the next level. And yet, you threw it all away because you liked writing pretty stories as if you were still seven years old."

"Just because you had a dream for me doesn't make yours objectively better than mine. In fact, it isn't, because mine is at least the dream I have for my own life. You've spent the last thirty years trying to get me to go into the law, because you think it's the right thing for me. But it isn't, and you won't listen when I tell you that. Now, I'm finally realizing my goals and aspirations, despite all the pressure you're putting on me, and you still can't even pretend to be happy for me? Wow."

"What is the point in pretending? So we can skirt around the issue rather than having a real conversation about it? No, I'm not happy for you, because you don't have perspective. You don't see what a long-term impact on your life this refusal to have a real career is going to have."

"And you do? If anyone here has lost perspective, it's you, the person who decided even before I was conceived what profession I was supposed to go into. And yet you can't handle the fact that maybe, just maybe, I want to live my own life. This is why I called, Mom. To let you know that while you think you gave me every chance, you made this harder for me. You fought me every single step of the way. You did your best to make sure I wasn't going to do what I wanted with the time I had on this earth. And guess what? I did it anyway. I have a contract. My first cheque from my advance. I'm going to be a real published author, and there's nothing you can do about it."

I finished my sentence and sighed. I hadn't wanted this conversation to go off the rails so quickly. Or at all. And yet, that was always what happened.

Why couldn't she just be happy for me? This was partly my fault. I knew, deep down, that there was no part of Mom that was ever going to just be glad I was living life on my own terms. But still, a little part of me still wanted to try.

"You're right. It is your life, and I can't stop you from making horrible decisions. But I can certainly try. Because here's the thing, Penelope: your decisions affect more than just you. Because you've always had this rebellious streak, you've refused to see it, but the choices you make affect our entire family."

"I'm sorry you have to go to the country club and admit to people that one of your children isn't a lawyer," I said dryly.

"It's more than just that," she snapped. "A family legacy, a family dynasty, it has to include the

Read Between the Lies

entire family. Your sisters are all lawyers. What happens if one of them decides to go into politics? What will happen when one of them comes up for partner? Do you really think it would look better to have an entire family of lawyers, or a family where there are mostly lawyers, but one of the daughters decides to go out on her own and be an artist?"

The ridicule with which my mom said the last word cut me to my core.

"I don't know, Mom. I think you're overestimating the reverence the general public has for lawyers."

"I don't care about the general public. I care about the elite in this country. The group of people your father and I worked so hard to join and where I will *not* allow my position to be ruined by a daughter who doesn't understand what family truly means."

"That's funny, given what happened between you and Dad."

"You do not get to speak to me that way. You don't understand what happened between us."

"Maybe not, but neither do any of your country-club friends. And I guarantee you they're judging you for leaving Dad a lot more than they are for having a child who isn't a lawyer. Go to therapy, Mom. I'm a human being. Your daughter. You're not playing some real-life version of *The Sims* where you're trying to get every person in your family to hit the top of the career ladder while ignoring the fact that they're breaking down sobbing in front of the mirror every night as you force them to practice their charisma."

"What on *earth* are you talking about?"

"A game I used to play. You know, for fun. Like real people do. And believe me, I get it. This doesn't actually have to do with my sisters. It has to do with you, your friends, and how you're embarrassed to have to admit to all your fancy lawyer pals when you have drinks in the conference room at nine pm on a Friday, pretending that you're about to have a weekend, that one of your children hasn't lived up to your own expectations. Well, guess what, Mom? I'm a signed author. I'm going to be successful. There will come a day when you're going to be *proud* to walk into that room and tell your colleagues that you gave birth to Poppy Perkins. A day when the driver of your car—because we all know you'd never be seen dead on public transit—will hold up one of my books and ask if you can get it autographed for them. And when that day comes, I know you won't apologize to me, because that's not your style. But I hope that at that moment, you realize that my success will be despite you, not because of you. And that you were wrong about me. Wrong about everything you've ever told me about the world. I know that will be hard for you, because you're incapable of ever admitting to being wrong. But you will be wrong. And I will not forgive you for it."

My phone trembled in my hand as I finished that sentence, and I realized when I got to the end of it that tears streamed down my face. I was crying.

"You see, this is ridiculous. You're living out this fantasy in your head."

"I'm just getting started living it, Mom."

"This conversation is pointless. I would congratulate you on your deal, but all it will do is allow you to continue this fantasy that you're going to be the next Stephen King."

"You're right. It is pointless. I don't know what I was thinking. Goodbye, Mom."

"I spoke with the head of admissions at Stanford the other day. You're still able to apply for law school there and be considered for the spring semester."

"Not interested."

"In that case, goodbye."

I ended the call and let the phone drop onto the mattress next to me. Tears stung my eyes, but they weren't entirely tears of sadness. That was there, without question. I knew not everyone was lucky enough to have parents that loved and supported them for who they were, but that didn't mean I wasn't allowed to feel crushing pain every time it was made obvious that that was the family I'd been born into.

There was more than that, though. There was rage. Rage that my mother, of all people, the person who was supposed to be there for me, supposed to support me, supposed to love me, wasn't doing that for me.

And a determination to prove her wrong. It wasn't just that she thought I was selfish, that I wasn't considering her feelings when she went to the country club and had to admit that one of her children hadn't gone into law. No. It was this idea she had that even if I could manage this, I wouldn't, because I was inherently not good enough.

Well, I was going to show her that I had it in me. I could be a successful author. Then even Mom would no longer be able to see me as a failure.

Maybe—just maybe—she'd even be proud of me.

Chapter 12

I PULLED OUT MY LAPTOP AND CONTINUED TO work on my book after that. I was newly inspired by the lack of faith a handful of people seemed to have in me. Francesca didn't think I'd ever finish this book at all. Mom thought that even if I did, my career as an author would never be successful. Juliette obviously thought I wasn't going to amount to anything, that I was enough of a nobody that she could straight-up steal from me.

Well, I was more than willing to prove them all wrong. I forced myself to keep writing, even when I didn't know exactly where I wanted the story to go. After all, the first step was to have something written down. Something could be edited. Bad words could be transformed into good words. But a blank page would never be more than just that: a blank page.

Eventually, I started yawning more than I was

typing, and I realized it was time to go to bed. I closed the laptop lid and slid under the covers, dreaming of the day that my book would be published.

I woke up feeling refreshed after a long, hard, emotional afternoon the day before. At least dinner with Nick had been nice. I got up, poured myself a bowl of cereal, and figured I had time to go downstairs and get a coffee before I went to Ophelia's. I couldn't wait to get rid of this sling; I couldn't ride my bike with just one arm—okay, I couldn't ride my bike *safely* with just one arm—and walking took so much longer.

I threw on some clothes—speaking of things that took longer these days—then grabbed my tote bag. I carefully ran my fingers over the typewriter enamel pin that always reminded me that above all, I was a writer, and headed downstairs.

Laura Belle was working behind the counter this morning.

"You're grinnin' like a possum that just ate a sweet tater," she said to me. "Feeling better today?"

"Lots," I said with a smile. "Yesterday sucked, but today is promising."

"I'm glad to hear it. Now you run along, and when you come back this afternoon and I've had a moment. I'm busier than a cat burying poop on a marble floor this morning."

"That's a mental image," I said with a laugh and

Read Between the Lies

a wave as I walked to the other end of the counter to wait for my order.

I grabbed my coffee from John when it was ready and began the walk down to Ophelia's office. I stepped into the elevator, and when I did, a man rushed in after me.

"Hold the door, please," he called out, his accent French. I did so and he rushed in after me. He wore a full suit, grey wool, obviously custom tailored. He brushed himself down, as if embarrassed that he'd dared to speed up a couple of steps to catch an elevator, looked at the button I'd pressed, then looked me up and down, not an ounce of shame.

"Excuse me, I am right here. I have a full cup of coffee, and I'm not afraid to use it," I warned him. I made sure to maintain eye contact with him. He was on the shorter side, maybe five foot seven, medium build, with a day's worth of stubble. His eyes were the same dark shade as his hair, like a strong shot of espresso, and his eyelashes were long. His aquiline nose stood out among his features, but he was far from ugly.

"You *Américaines*, you are so—what is the word— feisty. I have simply not seen you before, and you are obviously heading to Ophelia's office. You are her new secretary?"

"No, are you?" I replied. The man was obviously annoyed at my response—and my refusal to say more—and he scowled and turned back toward the door. I flipped him off behind his back as the doors opened.

"*Ophélia*," he called out, striding into the main hallway as if he owned the place. My friend emerged from her office, all smiles despite the man's obvious anger.

"Ah, Jean-Paul. It has been too long. Did you get my message?"

"You are not one to normally send me on—how do you say—a wild goose chase. I have come all the way from Lyon myself, with your assurance that the lost Kandinsky was located here."

Ophelia's smile dropped. "We were too late."

"No, the painting, it was there. Exactly where you said to look for it. However, it was not the real painting. It was a fake. You sent me here for a fake."

"No. Come on, Jean-Paul. You know me. When have I ever sent you after a fake?"

"Never. That is why, when I received your message, I came at once. Myself. With my best team. But the painting we took, it was a fake. There is nothing we can do now. No prosecution. You have wasted my time, and a whole team, for what is not even a good fake."

"He moved it before you got here, then. Come on, Jean-Paul. Don't be an idiot. It doesn't look good on you. It is one thing for me to fall for a good fake, but do you really think I would have fallen for a bad one?"

"No," Jean-Paul admitted, and he became

slightly less animated. "But in the end, it is all the same to me. I have no painting. I return to France empty-handed. I thought it was the lost Kandinsky, at last."

"It's still here," Ophelia replied. "Somewhere. It's in the city. He wouldn't have moved it far."

"Did you really have to tell him you knew about it?" Jean-Paul said with a sigh.

"Yes. I needed the leverage against him."

"No, you needed to let him know how much smarter you are than him."

"That should have been obvious from the start."

"It is your problem, Ophelia. You do not know when to stay quiet."

"No, I said exactly what I meant to say to get the information I needed. You forget I don't work for Interpol. I never have, officially. I have different goals to you."

"Everyone should have the goal of bringing great artwork back to the places who own it."

"I don't disagree with you, but some things are more important. And in this case, it means bringing a murderer to justice."

"And have you succeeded?"

"Not yet."

"Which means that I have lost the painting I was promised was in that man's office, and you still have not solved your case," Jean-Paul said. "Well, at least neither one of us is happy."

"With such a defeatist attitude, how do you ever

find anything? I told you I haven't succeeded *yet*. I will. And you? What are you doing now?"

Jean-Paul shrugged in a way that was somehow very distinctly French. "*Bien*, I have nothing else to do. The painting, it is gone. I get back on the plane to France."

"You aren't going to investigate?"

"My boss did not believe me when I told him the lost Kandinsky had been found in an office in San Francisco. I told him my source was trustworthy. He put faith in me and sent me out with a team. However, when I reported to him that it was a fake, he told me to get back to France. There are other important cases of art theft that require my assistance. Did you hear about the theft in Belgium the other week?"

"Of course."

"Three hundred million American dollars' worth of diamonds, stolen in one night. Very brazen robbery, and yet we are nowhere. You should come back and work for us again."

A small smile flickered in the corners of Ophelia's mouth. "Absolutely not."

"Things are different now."

"That's what they all say."

"I mean it. The ones who are left, we know you were telling the truth."

"And yet you didn't believe it when I told you. It was only when I proved it. I only work with people who believe me now. And I'm much happier for it. So this Kandinsky, Interpol is out?"

Jean-Paul opened his palms. "That decision, it is out of my hands. I must return to France. You should not have told the owner of the painting that you knew it was real."

Ophelia shrugged. "I did what I thought was best."

"You simply have never learned that what you think is best and what actually is best are not always the same thing."

"This is why I don't work for Interpol."

Jean-Paul shook his head. "It has, as always, been very nice to see you, Ophelia. And frustrating. It is always frustrating."

"Lovely to see you, too, dear."

"Please let me know the next time you are in Lyon."

"I will."

Jean-Paul turned then, without giving me so much as another glance, and he headed toward the elevator, shaking his head. When he'd entered and the old-fashioned clock-style mechanism above the door began its slow stutter to the left, I turned to Ophelia.

"I guess Kyle didn't believe your promise."

"I didn't think he would. But I will admit, I thought it would take him longer to get rid of it than it would for me to get an Interpol team over here."

"You're right, though. Either way, you made the right call. I like art, and I think it's important—obviously, given as I'm a writer, but there's not a single piece of art in this world that's worth more than a human life."

Ophelia nodded. "Yes, I agree. Unfortunately, Jean-Paul has fallen victim to the blindness which often accompanies one giving everything they have into their job. He is an excellent thief hunter, but unfortunately, it's turned him into a slightly worse human. But that's all right. We can't all hunt murderers. Then no art would ever be found."

"So, what happens now? We can't just give up on that painting, can we?"

"No," Ophelia said with a smile. "We won't give up on it. How do you feel about felonies?"

"I grew up in a house with lawyers. In general, I'm opposed."

"And in practice?"

"I mean, I guess it depends on the specific felony."

"Stealing a piece of art to return it to its rightful owner from a thief. Hypothetically."

"Do you think the two crimes cancel each other out?"

"It's not about what I think."

"One of the reasons why I didn't want to go into law was that I very quickly discovered, growing up, that the law and justice were not always one and the same. In fact, most of the time, they took converging courses. I always thought we should strive for justice. And in this case, getting the stolen property to its rightful owner so they can put it back on display and allow as many people as possible to see it in its true glory—that sounds like justice to me."

"So you're in?"

"Are you asking if I'm willing to commit a felony to get a fifty-million-dollar painting back to its rightful owner?"

"Yes. Hypothetically."

"I am. No hypothetical needed."

"Good."

"Where do we start? We don't know where the painting is, after all, if it's no longer at his office."

"That's true. We need to find out where he took it, and then, we'll take it back. Interpol actually showing up will have scared Kyle enough that he'll need to nick down to the shops for a fresh pair of pants. He won't bring the original back to the office for a while; he'll want to keep it hidden. He'll want to lie low."

"Right. It won't be at his home, because he's going to figure Interpol could find that pretty quickly. He'll want to hide it somewhere, preferably somewhere that can't be traced back to him."

"Yes. We have to find out where it went, and for that, we need Fiona."

"She's not going to enjoy you calling her again," I said wryly.

169

"Oh, I don't think I'm going to have to," Ophelia replied with a mischievous smile. "Now, come on. Let's go to my office; I want you to run through everything Steph told you last night once again."

Chapter 13

"It was right outside my apartment," I told her. "She said she'd been in the area, and she spotted me. She was going to come here in the morning, but when she saw me alone, she wanted to get it off her chest. I got the impression she was really nervous about it. She didn't want to tattle on Oliver, but in the end, her sense of right and wrong took over. Plus, I don't know this firsthand, but I imagine it's hard to sleep at night, wondering if the guy snoring next to you is willing to stab someone in cold blood in the middle of the street."

Ophelia shrugged. "You get used to it."

"Normal people don't," I pointed out.

"Okay, that is a good point."

"Anyway, she came up to me and started rambling. I eventually got it all out of her. She said that Ellie and Oliver had been working together for months, cheating at chess. They didn't meet two months ago, like Oliver said. It had been going on for longer."

"Did you ask whether it was entirely platonic?"

"I did. She insisted it was and that she wasn't simply saying that out of naivety. She considered it a risk and looked out for signs that it was happening, but she didn't see any."

"Did she tell you how they were doing it?"

"A hidden computer inside Ellie's things. A notebook. She would tap the moves made, and the computer would tell her what to do next. She would then blink the response to Oliver in a code they'd come up with."

"It had to be something like that. And it worked, since no one in the chess world would have known Ellie and Oliver knew each other."

"Exactly. A few days before she was killed, though, Ellie had been recognized. Someone from college saw her in the crowd of a game and contacted her. She thought the risk was too high that she'd be found after basically disappearing from the math world forever."

Ophelia nodded. "I imagine the chess world and the math world have some overlap."

"Right. So Ellie told Oliver she was out; she wasn't going to help him cheat at chess anymore, and he lost it. Steph said Oliver smashed a vase against the wall and that she replaced it with the brown one that's there now."

Read Between the Lies

"The brown one? You're sure that's what she said?"

"Yeah. Why does it matter?"

"It may mean nothing." Ophelia motioned for me to continue.

"Anyway, she said that the day Ellie was murdered, Oliver was in a mood. She chalked it up to residual upset over Ellie quitting their scheme, but then she began to wonder."

"It's certainly interesting," Ophelia said.

"Oliver was always a suspect, but now we've got good motive for him too."

"And he had the opportunity; he was at home alone when Ellie was killed."

"Right. As far as I'm concerned, he's at the top of the suspect list. But we're still going to meet with Anna Mayer, right?"

"We are," Ophelia confirmed. "We're lucky that she happens to be in the city for a promotional tour this week. We're meeting her in her hotel room in about an hour. And until then, we wait for the next person to be involved in our heist to arrive."

"I spoke with my mom last night. Told her about my book deal."

Ophelia raised an eyebrow. "How did it go?"

"I mean, I'm not going to say well. It was never going to go well. But it went about the way I thought it would. I told myself I wasn't going to lose it on her, and then she made it all about her, and I kind of did.

But I'm proud of myself for doing that too. Because Mom said I was being selfish, and I was ruining the good family name, but I don't think that's true."

Ophelia snorted. "You're joking, right? Ruining the family name?"

"I know. She said if any of my sisters came up for a SCOTUS nomination or something, they'd look into our family, and it would look better if we were all lawyers. Like somehow, being a writer is a shameful thing."

Ophelia shook her head. "Not a chance in the world."

"Right. And I know that isn't her real motivation. Mom just doesn't want to have to face people at her lawyers' meetings and tell them that one of her children didn't follow her into the law. It's ultimately all about her."

"Yes. Half the presidents of this country have siblings who have done far worse than dare to write books for a living. Your mother is out to lunch."

"So, I told her that. And I might have also landed a low blow by telling her if the people at her clubs are talking about anything in her life, it's the divorce with Dad and not what I'm doing."

Ophelia winced. "Ouch, that would have hurt."

"Yeah. She brushed it off, like she always does, but the conversation ended pretty quickly after that. But it's fine. I'm honestly used to it. It hurts, and I'd love to have a more normal mom, but it is what it is."

"If I've learned one thing in life, it's that there are very few people who are actually normal. My mom wasn't, either, although she was a bit different to yours."

"Look, we haven't known each other for very long, but there's not a single part of your life that I believe has ever been normal."

Ophelia laughed good-naturedly. "That's a fair assessment. It helps that I think normality is overrated."

"Me too, but it would still be nice to get a normal hug from a normal mom one day. Or even to be able to tell her I got stabbed in the shoulder and have her come over to make me chicken soup or something. Is that what normal moms do? I don't even know anymore."

"I can understand that desire, for sure."

"But it's fine. I know I need to stop obsessing. Really, I should cut her off completely, but I can't bring myself to do that. At least I have Lily and Laura Belle. They're basically my adoptive mothers. How about you? How's your relationship with your mother?"

Before Ophelia had a chance to respond, the elevator doors opened once more. Ophelia and I got up and headed to the hallway, where Fiona was heading casually toward us. Today, she was dressed in a gorgeous sweater with slim-fitting jeans and kitten heels.

"Good morning, Fiona," Ophelia said sweetly.

"Oh, don't give me that crap," Fiona replied. "You and I both know why I'm here. Good morning, Poppy."

"Hi, Fiona."

"You're bored, and you want something to do," Ophelia said.

"I mean, you seem like you're stuck here. You obviously need me, and I'm a good friend. This is what good friends do."

"You're absolutely correct. I do need help, always."

"I've told my husband I'm involved in a new charity that's growing and needs my time. He thinks I'm doing administrative work for you."

"Well, in a way, you will be."

"So, what's happening now?"

"A Kandinsky was stolen from a museum in Portugal seventeen years ago. Do you remember that happening?"

"No, because I'm not a complete weirdo like you who remembers every single tiny thing they've ever read about in the paper."

"Well, it happened, and the painting was never seen again. Until Poppy and I found it yesterday afternoon in the lobby of a private equity firm owned by Kyle Wellman."

A small smile grew in the corner of Fiona's mouth. "Ballsy."

"It certainly was. But by the time Jean-Paul

arrived and got his team into the office, the Kandinsky had disappeared."

"Oh, don't tell me you actually told the guy you knew what he had."

"I had to. We were trying to find a killer. That is the priority."

"Okay, that's fair."

"Anyway, because Jean-Paul has been recalled to Lyon, with his boss likely thinking I'm a hysterical woman who saw a copy of the painting and reported it as the truth, we're on our own. I want that Kandinsky back."

Fiona smiled. "How much of this is about getting the painting back, and how much of it is about proving to Kyle that you're not to be messed with?"

Ophelia twisted her wrist a few times. "Oh, about fifty-fifty."

"Good." Then Fiona turned to me. "When Ophelia gets about seventy-thirty revenge, that's when you need to watch out, because she starts making stupid moves just to get what she wants."

"They're not stupid. They're calculated risks."

"They're risks, all right."

"Calculated."

"You're not as good at math as you think you are."

"I am excellent at math."

"See?"

The two friends stared each other down for a moment.

"Okay," I finally interrupted. "Point is, this isn't a super-risky situation. Not yet. So, Ophelia, what do you need Fiona to do for us, exactly?"

"Are you going to be involved in this?" Fiona asked me.

"Yeah."

"Aren't you from a family of famous lawyers?"

"Yes."

"So how do I know you're not going to leave here and immediately go to the cops?"

"I'm not my family. I'm not a lawyer, and Ophelia here obviously trusts me not to do that. Besides, I haven't had the best experience with the police here in San Francisco. I've also spent more than enough time with Ophelia to know that even if I did, she'd probably be able to wriggle out of any charges, anyway. Sameen is very good."

"She is," Ophelia confirmed.

"All right," Fiona said, obviously satisfied with my answer. "I'm in. What are we doing?"

"I need to find out where that painting is hidden."

"A painting that was stolen seventeen years ago and has disappeared from an office sometime in the last twenty-four hours."

"On the bright side, we now know what city it's in."

Read Between the Lies

"Yeah, should be a piece of cake," Fiona said, rolling her eyes.

"If anyone can do this, it's you. Besides, you came here because you're bored as hell. This is a challenge."

"What are you going to do when you find out where the painting is? There are three of us. And we both know I'm better on the outside of things. Are the two of you really going to be able to do this on your own?"

"There are four of us," Ophelia corrected. "Sameen will help with any legal issues that pop up. But she won't commit any crimes herself. For now, it's Poppy and me. We'll see what you find out and go from there. I was thinking about calling Taylor."

Fiona propped a single eyebrow skyward. "Taylor? Really?"

"She's very good at this sort of thing."

"She's a psychopath."

"All the better to commit a crime with. Besides, she's not a psychopath. She's low-key insane. There's a difference."

"She almost got us all killed back in Colombia that one time."

"We're still here, though. She got it under control in the end."

"I didn't realize she was in town."

"She moved here a year ago. This town attracts people with ambition."

"Taylor always had that," Fiona said.

"Anyway, it's not settled yet. We need to know what we're dealing with, first. Poppy and I are going to interview Anna Mayer."

"Okay. I'll see you when you get back."

Fiona flashed me a smile, which I returned, as Ophelia and I headed to the elevator while Fiona went into what was now her office.

Who knew that solving a murder might only be the second most interesting thing I was going to do today?

Chapter 14

"Given what I'm finding out about the people you know, I'm starting to wonder about me," I said as we climbed into Ophelia's Audi sedan.

"Oh?"

"Every single person you know seems to be insane, in some way. And seeing as I've been spending more and more time with you, that apparently includes me."

"People who aren't seen as crazy by the outside world rarely ever change it."

"So, you're saying you think I'm nuts too."

"By your definition, yes. Absolutely. Look at you. You're a nearly thirty-year-old woman who has defied her family's expectations by chasing your dreams. Not only that, but you've worked hard enough to begin achieving them. When you were suspected of a murder, you set about solving it, and now you're about to try and solve a second. We can pretend it's out of a sense of duty to a woman you barely knew, but that would be a lie, wouldn't it? You're doing it because you're interested. You want to solve the puzzle, same as I do. And yes, by your definition, that makes you as crazy as the rest of us." Ophelia shot me a smile. "But don't worry. That's not a bad thing. Normality is overrated."

I mulled her words over for a while. "I suppose we always like to see ourselves as normal."

"You're right. And perspective is everything in life. Embrace the fact that you aren't what you would consider to be 'normal.' Life is much more interesting that way."

"One person's interesting is another person's life of crime."

"I solve more crimes than I commit. I figure that tips the scales in my favor."

I laughed. "That's one way of looking at it."

It didn't take long before we reached the Stanford Court Hotel, halfway up Nob Hill on California Street. Located at the corner where three lines of cable cars met, the site of the hotel had originally been the home of Leland Stanford's mansion. One of the most expensive private properties ever built at the time, it was destroyed in the 1908 earthquake. Some of the most luxurious apartments in San Francisco were built on the site, and in 1968, it was purchased and redeveloped as a five-star hotel.

Ophelia parked the car, and we entered the

hotel, the lobby a mixture of old-world charm and modern touches. We headed to the elevators, whose slight creaks and groans betrayed the building's history but only added to the hotel's charm. The next thing I knew, we were knocking on Anna Mayer's dark-blue door, which opened a moment later.

Anna Mayer was short; no more than five foot one, with a slim frame and curious dark eyes that darted between Ophelia and me. Her almost-black hair was cut in a stylish bob that framed her face. She was dressed casually, in a pair of sweatpants and an oversized sweater.

"Hello, Anna. I am Ophelia. We spoke on the phone earlier."

"Yes, yes. Come in," Anna said, opening the door and motioning for us to enter. Her voice held the slightest trace of an Austrian accent.

The interior walls were a crisp beige, with black-and-gold carpet adding a touch of color. The décor was without question mid-century modern. We were led into a living room with a sectional and chair facing the television, and a small, round table and chairs in the far corner made up the dining room. An open doorway set in the far wall led to the bedroom.

"Have a seat," Anna said, motioning to the couch while she took the chair. "When I heard from you the other day, I did not know what to think. You are investigating the murder of Ellie

Jacobs. And yet, why do you need to speak to me?"

"Because the two of you were together," Ophelia said softly. It wasn't a question, it was a statement. "She was your girlfriend."

Anna swallowed hard, and tears immediately welled in her eyes, which glistened slightly. "How do you know?" Her voice was small, not much more than a whisper.

"It started with a photo in a newspaper article," Ophelia explained. "The game where you defeated Oliver Dorchester, a few months ago. Everyone was looking at him, at his move, except her. I suspected something then. So, I went back, and I found footage of her at your games. The way she was looking at you, she was more than just a fan."

Anna nodded. "She was. I suppose there is no harm in admitting it now. Ellie wanted to keep our relationship a secret. She didn't want people from her former life, when she was in mathematics, to find her. There is a lot of overlap between the chess community and the math community."

"I can imagine," I said. "How did you meet her?"

"It was about a month before I beat Dorchester, at another chess tournament. We ended up at the same bar. We began to chat and hit it off straight away. She was fun. We both knew it would be a diffi-cult relationship—chess has me travelling most of the year, and my primary residence is still in Austria

—but after that tournament, we decided to try and make it work all the same. Long-distance relationships are so much simpler these days, after all. FaceTime and everything."

"How serious were things between the two of you?"

"We were moving fast," Anna admitted. "We had started talking about me moving permanently to San Francisco. That's one of the reasons I am here, in fact. Officially, it is a trip to promote one of my sponsors, a jewelry company whose products I wear while I play. But unofficially, I was apartment hunting as well. A week ago, I'd finally made that call. I wanted to live here, be closer to Ellie, permanently."

"Did you know that Ellie had been working with Oliver Dorchester?"

Anna frowned. "Working with? Oliver? How do you mean?"

"If I told you Ellie was helping him cheat, would that surprise you?"

Anna furrowed her brow for a moment. I was surprised, to be honest. I'd have thought she'd have jumped to Ellie's defense, immediately refuted the accusation. But she took it seriously.

"Surprise? No. Is that really what was happening? Ellie was working with Oliver?"

"It's why she was at the game, watching. Likely why she was at the same bar as all the other chess players that night too."

"So Dorchester is cheating." Anna said it in a very matter-of-fact way, as if she was stating the day's weather.

"Yes. How does that make you feel?"

"Glad."

"Glad?" I asked. "Really?"

Anna grinned at me. "I'm still better than he is, even when he cheats. I bet that hurts. He hates me."

"Because of your relationship with Ellie?" I asked.

Anna shook her head. "Oh no, he's hated me long before her. I don't know if Oliver would have even known the two of us were dating. Do you know if Ellie mentioned our relationship?"

"We don't," I admitted. "And he didn't say anything."

"Then he didn't know. Oliver wasn't a discreet person. He would have told you if he knew."

"Did you resent the fact that Ellie was hiding your relationship from the world?"

"Not in the least. I know her history. I assume the two of you do as well?"

Ophelia and I both nodded.

"Then you understand why she wanted to keep away from anything that might have connected her to her former life as a prodigal mathematician."

"Why would she help Oliver, then?" I asked. "After all, wouldn't it have been safer for her to stay away from chess tournaments?"

"Ellie still loved math. She loved puzzles. She

loved to solve problems. I bet you whatever she was doing with Oliver, however she was cheating with him, she would have come up with the idea. She would have executed it. And she would have been careful not to be seen. She wanted a piece of this life back, but she wanted it on her terms."

"You don't seem upset that she was helping Oliver," I pointed out.

"For one thing, I have only your word for it. I can't ask Ellie what she was actually doing. I can't ask her the reasons behind it if you're really telling me the truth. But I know what things were like between us. I know our relationship was strong. Let me guess: next you'll insinuate that she and Oliver were also together, and that she was cheating on me."

"Do you think she was?" Ophelia asked.

"No, of course not. Ellie was bisexual. I know that. And she and Oliver had had a bit of a fling when she was in college; she told me about that as well. But I fully trusted her. And I knew her. If she was helping him, it was for a love of math, not for a love of him."

"For what it's worth, she told him she wasn't going to help him anymore," Ophelia said. "A couple of weeks ago."

"Right when I said I'd move to San Francisco to be with her," Anna said slowly.

"It looks like Ellie was committing to your relationship," Ophelia said.

"How did Oliver take it? It can't have been well. If Ellie was helping him cheat, especially if she's the one who came up with the method to do it, his whole career is over."

"She hasn't been helping him long enough for his entire score to be a sham," Ophelia said. "Oliver can obviously play chess. He might just be tenth in the world, instead of third."

"That's still quite a drop. That should be fun to watch."

"Why does he hate you?" I asked. "He's obviously competitive, but you specifically seem to get under his skin."

"It happens a lot. Men who pretend they're allies. They say all the right things. Insist that it's completely fine that women are in their field and succeeding, doing better than they are. But when it comes down to it, they can't handle it. Oliver is like that. It's misogyny."

"You're very casual about it," I pointed out.

"I'm one of very few women in a very male-dominated field. Frankly, the fact that Oliver even attempted a thin veil of allyship is more than many of my competitors bother with. There are a few who I believe are genuinely happy to see women succeed, but they're certainly not the majority."

"Do you know who could have killed Ellie?" Ophelia asked.

"Given what you've told me, I assume you've looked at Oliver."

Read Between the Lies

"We have."

"He'd be the only person on my list."

"Did Ellie have any problems at work?"

Anna pursed her lips. "Nothing out of the ordinary. Nothing worth killing over. She'd accidentally taken someone else's lunch one day, and the woman whose food she ate was very upset, but it was easily sorted out. Those are the kinds of issues Ellie had at work. She was liked by her coworkers, as far as she let me know. I can't think of anyone there who would want her dead. Or anywhere. Ellie was sweet. I really liked her. I think I even loved her."

"I'm very sorry for your loss," Ophelia said.

"Thank you. At least Ellie had told her family about me. They've been in touch about funeral arrangements. I'll be able to go to that, at least. I suppose there's no reason to hide our relationship anymore. There's no risk to Ellie that anyone from her past would recognize her and make things difficult for her again. She was so worried about that. But she didn't want to let what happened to her in the past ruin her future too. When I met her, she wore a blond wig and did her makeup differently than normal. She eventually showed me who she really was and explained why she had to hide her identity. I understood. I was willing to do whatever it took to be with her, even if it meant hiding the fact that we were dating from the rest of the chess world."

"Plus, I imagine the disguise would have helped

prevent anybody linking her with Oliver," I muttered.

"I wish she was here so I could ask her about that," Anna said, a touch of pain in her voice. "But I get it. Ellie was happy in her job. She really enjoyed it. But I think she needed more. She needed math. She was so good at it. I've never seen anything like it. I studied math in school, and if I'd gone to university instead of focusing on chess, it's what I would have done. But Ellie played with numbers like they were hers to command. She was incredible."

"There's no one else you can think of that could have wanted Ellie dead?" Ophelia asked softly.

"No. No, there isn't. Are you sure this wasn't a random attack?"

"We aren't, but we're operating under the assumption that it wasn't."

"Okay. Thank you for looking into Ellie's death. I appreciate it."

"Of course."

Ophelia and I stood, and Anna led us to the door. There was pain in her eyes as she said goodbye to us.

"What do you think?" Ophelia asked me when we got back into her car.

"I don't know," I said slowly. "On the one hand, everything she told us backs up what we know. If anything, it makes the case against Oliver even stronger. It seems to tie up a lot of the loose ends."

"Yes, it does, doesn't it," Ophelia said slowly. "Everything seems to fit in a nice, perfect puzzle against Oliver."

"So he did it, right?"

"Well, I'm not entirely certain of that just yet."

"What more do we need?"

"Right now, all we have is a story. And I can see the appeal, to you especially. The story is perfect and pretty. It has a beginning, a middle, and an end. But it's missing something."

"A little bit of mess. Because real life isn't like books, and there's always something messy involved."

"Exactly right. It's almost too perfect, isn't it?"

"So you're going to look the gift horse in the mouth."

"I've always hated that expression. There is exactly one example of a famously gifted horse, and looking inside its mouth would have very much changed the ending of that story."

"That's a very good point," I conceded.

"I don't want to jump to conclusions. We learned a lot of facts today. It's time to put them in their proper place. Although sometimes that feels like trying to herd cats on cocaine."

I laughed. "Yeah, I feel that. It would be nice if we had some sort of physical evidence. Like the murder weapon."

"Would you like a winning lottery ticket while you're at it?" Ophelia asked with a grin.

"I mean, I wouldn't say no. But I get it. The knife is probably somewhere at the bottom of San Francisco Bay right now."

"I wonder," Ophelia said quietly. "I wonder a lot of things."

Oliver Dorchester was obviously the prime suspect in this case. I just didn't know how we were going to prove it was him.

Chapter 15

When we got back to the office and passed by Fiona's work space, she called out to us.

"Meet me in the conference room in two. I have a whole lot to show you, and you're not going to want to miss it."

I had just enough time to get settled when Fiona entered the room behind us, holding a laptop in one hand, which she immediately connected to the projector on the far wall.

"What have you got?"

"A location," Fiona said with a self-satisfied smile. "Let me show you what I've found out."

She tapped the keys a couple of times and the projector screen changed to what was obviously security camera footage. It covered the front of the building where Kyle Wellman's company was located.

"This is from one thirty this morning," Ophelia

explained as she pressed Play on her keyboard. Nothing happened on the screen for a few seconds —the financial district wasn't exactly a high-traffic area during the middle of the night—but eventually, an unmarked white van pulled directly in front of the entrance to the building. Nobody emerged from the vehicle for about a minute, then the driver got out and pulled the rear doors of the van open.

About fifteen seconds later, two men emerged from the building, carrying a wrapped item that was suspiciously the same size of that Kandinsky.

"That's got to be it, right?" Fiona asked.

"I think so," Ophelia said. "I can't completely discount the idea that he might have swapped out the paintings and that this is a ruse, but I don't think so."

"Given the lengths this van went to so that I wouldn't be able to follow it, I agree. The real painting is going to be in here. And I also covered the rear exits. This is it."

"So where did he go?" I asked.

"Well, that's where things get interesting. I figured from where he goes, he has a few options. He could take the bridge across to Oakland pretty easily. That same route makes the most sense if he's heading south too. I've also covered north, since his personal home is up in Richmond Hill."

"And?"

"The driver didn't go for any of those. They

were obviously hoping to lose me by going through a bunch of residential neighborhoods."

"Where there wouldn't be as many CCTV cameras," I said, nodding.

"Right. But that's where they screwed up. Do you know how many doorbell cameras there are out there?"

"A lot."

"Exactly. They've exploded in popularity. It's estimated that twenty percent of American households have a doorbell camera now. Here in San Francisco, where people tend to adopt new technology quickly, that figure is even higher. It means with access to that footage, a person can essentially create a network of cameras that can survey entire neighborhoods."

"That's mildly unsettling, in a robots-are-taking-over-the-world kind of way."

"It is. And there's more risk than that too. The police have asked for—and received—footage from some doorbell camera companies without a warrant."

"How fun," I replied.

"Yes. However, in this particular situation, it's going to be to our advantage. Kyle thought he could lose any trace of where he drove by crossing through residential neighborhoods and avoiding commercial zones where CCTV footage was common, but it doesn't work that way. In fact, his new route made it even easier for me to follow; all I had to do was gain backend access into a network of doorbell cameras."

"Your skills as a hacker will never cease to amaze me," Ophelia said. "Great thinking and also great work."

"I'll be honest. I got the idea from another hacker, a few years ago," Fiona replied. "It was right when these things started getting popular. He said one day, and one day soon, they'd be used as mass surveillance devices without our knowledge, and he was right. Polka usually is."

"Polka?" I asked. "As in polka dot?"

Fiona shrugged. "I guess so. I don't know much about him, beyond the fact that he's considered to be one of the best hackers in the world, if not the very best. He doesn't talk about himself much, obviously. Anyway, using a combination of doorbell cams, I was able to trace the path the vehicle took through downtown. It eventually doubled back around down to a warehouse in Bayview. I know where that painting is. More or less."

"I'm not sure I like the sound of that last sentence," Ophelia said.

"I've narrowed it down to one of two possible warehouses. The truck was slowing down past one security camera, never passed the next one, and went back the way it came from ten minutes later. That left four doors it could have gone into, but I looked into the owners of those warehouses. I ruled out two of them. So it's not perfect, but come on.

That painting's been missing for seventeen years. I've given you three warehouses to look at; it's not that bad."

"No, good work," Ophelia said with a smile. "What's the address?"

Fiona rattled off a street name I didn't recognize. Bayview was a primarily industrial area at the south end of town, home to a number of old warehouses that I was sure would eventually get torn down in the name of building more overpriced condos. I was aware of it, but I'd never had any reason to find myself down there.

Fiona pulled up Google Street View, and I had a look. It was a dead-end street, with a drab, brown building on one side and an only slightly less drab building painted a combination of beige and grey on the other. Low-quality graffiti that was obviously more about the act than the art dotted the side of the building. The road was uneven. Cracks ran across it like spiderwebs, interspersed with a few potholes that looked like they could swallow up a medium-sized sedan.

A handful of cars and vans were parked along the edge of the white and beige building. A roller door set a few feet above the ground offered access into each warehouse, with concrete steps leading to rusted old doors next to each.

On the other side were only roller doors, nothing else.

"The painting is in one of these," Fiona said,

using her mouse to circle three roller doors. "Number 7 in the brown building and numbers 14 and 16 in the grey and white."

"Excellent," Ophelia said. "It will be dangerous and risky. I presume you will have to be at home with your family in the middle of the night?"

"I will," Fiona replied, and I couldn't help but hear the note of regret in her voice. "A fifty-million-dollar lost Kandinsky, and I'm going to have to sleep through its rescue."

"Oh, well. There will be lots of other opportunities to return stolen masterpieces to their rightful owners, I'm sure. Thank you for the help, Fiona. We're going to meet back here at eleven o'clock, Poppy. I should have a completed plan by then. We'll run through it, and then we're going to get that painting back without being arrested. All in a day's work."

"Okay. I have to get back home, but have fun," Fiona said, her voice giving the slight impression that she was pouting.

"We will. Although it would help to have someone like you there, I completely understand that you can't do it."

"If something should happen to come up, I'll let you know."

"Great."

Fiona waved goodbye at me and headed back into the hallway and toward the elevator. When I heard the doors close and the whirr of the mechanism sending it downward, I turned to Ophelia and grinned. "She's totally going to be here, isn't she?"

"Without question. This is who Fiona is, as much as she tries to hide it. I do believe people can change, but they have to want to change, in the depths of their core. Fiona convinced herself she wanted a different life, but deep down she doesn't."

"And we don't have anything to do for our murder case yet, right?"

"Correct. I think we have a lot of the necessary information. I just need some time to sort through it all in my head. I don't think we'll have anything to act on together until tomorrow."

"Okay, cool. I'll see you tonight, then."

I left the office and headed back out into the street. It was early afternoon. I had lots of time to go home and have a nap before eleven, and I wanted to write some more of my book.

The thing was, Francesca's words had lit a fire under my ass, but they'd also terrified me. Deep down, as much as I wanted this, I also knew she was right: I was a new author who had never fully written a book before. The book had been sold on spec, which was rare in the publishing world, but Ellie had loved it and fought for it.

Francesca didn't believe in me, though. Like my mother, she thought I was destined for failure. And while I was going to do everything I could to prove her wrong, there was always that niggling voice in the back of my head, asking whether or not I really could do it.

What if they were right? What if Francesca had me nailed down? I wasn't a writer. What if Mom was right? I was going to fail at this. I wasn't going to be a famous author. Hell, I wasn't even going to be a mid-list author. What if I couldn't get the book finished?

No. I forcefully threw the thought aside. I refused to accept that. I was going to do it. I had to do it. This was the first step toward everything I wanted in life, and I wasn't about to trip and fall onto my face. Not this early.

I almost headed straight home but took a quick detour to The Shop Formerly Known as STD. After all, Jenny planned on opening in the morning, and I wanted to see how it was going.

When I reached the storefront, I audibly gasped. The windows, which used to have a decal that read San Techcisco Donuts in the ultra-modern sans serif font Elana had used, had been replaced with a very classically French-looking font that read La Bonne Bouche. They were still covered with newspaper, but I knocked on the door, and a moment later, Jenny opened it.

When she saw me, she grinned. "I'm so glad you're here. I know you're going to see the place tomorrow, but I desperately want you to see it now. Come on in."

I stepped over the threshold and into the store, and my breath caught in my throat.

"Wow, Jenny," was all I managed to say. This place looked like a perfect French bakery. The pale pink walls were offset by the new long counter, which was white and farmhouse style. She had re-painted all the tables white and all the chairs a robin's egg blue that acted as a great accent against all the pink and white. A few had been replaced with upholstered light gray wingback chairs. The glossy white subway tiles of the back wall were gorgeous. Gold and black accents dotted the store. The wall on the right was decorated with gold-framed mirrors, which did a great job of reflecting the light, making the whole space appear brighter than it used to. This shop had gone from a sterile store that looked like a Dunkin' Donuts wannabe to a cute, comfortable space where I knew people would want to spend time.

"Does that mean you like it?"

"I know this is a total cliché, but I don't just like it—I love it! This looks fantastic. It's so inviting and open."

Jenny nodded. "That's exactly what I was going for. And it actually didn't end up being that bad, in terms of turnover. I didn't want the store to be closed for a month while I changed everything up. I'm trying to get as much of the old staff back as possible, and obviously none of us want to go a month without getting paid."

"You got it all done so quickly. I'm really impressed."

"Thanks. I repurposed as much of everything as I could. The tables and chairs are the same. I just covered the back kitchen in plastic sheeting and went to town with spray paint. The coffee machine is the same, I got the tiles at a discount, and the mirrors all came from a second-hand store. I just spray-painted the frames as well. The counter is new, but it was in stock at a local hardware store. I had a friend come and trim it to fit around the donut display shelves, which I've kept the same. Most of the little accents on the shelves here and there are also from the second-hand store, except for the succulents, which came from my place. And of course, I painted."

"You're Superwoman."

"Superwoman takes a lot of Advil, then. I feel both so incredibly energized and like I could sleep for three days straight. Which is kind of a weird combination of feelings, but that's how it's going. I've got about an hour of details left to sort out, and then I'm taking the newspaper down off the window, and tomorrow morning, we're going to be open. Are you ready?"

"Sure am," I said with a grin. I didn't mention that I'd probably be running on about three hours of sleep. It was going to be fine.

"I'm so glad to hear it. How's everything going with your book? And the murder?"

I shrugged. "Well, the book is okay. My new editor, well, it's a work in progress."

Jenny frowned. "That bad, huh? Well, even Tolkien had an editor he had to work with. Presumably?"

"I love that you know to ask me about *Lord of the Rings*. I'm not sure they had the greatest relationship," I said with a grin. "I know at one point they tried to get Tolkien to change 'dwarfs' and 'elfs' to 'dwarves' and 'elves,' which was grammatically correct, but it was fantasy! Which of course wasn't really a genre at the time. They were more like copy editors than developmental ones. He pretty much just did what he wanted."

"Is that what you want?"

"Yes and no. Probably more no. Francesca is right. I'm a new author who's never published anything before. I'm not arrogant enough to think I'm going to do everything correctly the first time around. I'm going to do my best, obviously, but I think having someone behind me who can help make changes to turn it into a great book will be helpful."

"That's probably a good call."

"Life's changing fast for all of us, it looks like."

"It sure is. I don't think the pressure of what taking over this place means has really sunk in for me yet. I'm probably going to show up tomorrow and look for Elana to tell me what to do."

"Yeah. I know exactly what you mean."

"I want to try to find a place to live that's closer to town too. Right now, I'm still living with my mom in Oakland, but I want to be close enough to this place that if there's an emergency, I can be there within a few minutes, instead of being at least half an hour away on a good day."

"What are you looking for?"

Jenny shrugged. "I mean, it's San Francisco. I'm not getting a three-bedroom house for myself. Not that I need that either. I'd be happy with almost anything."

"Did I tell you that Juliette left my place? I'm looking for a roommate. It's not big, and we'd be practically sleeping on top of one another, but it's a room just a few blocks from here. It comes out to just under a grand a month each, and there's a small storage area on the ground floor where you can keep a bike, which is really handy."

"Plus, I'm already at least eighty percent sure you're not a serial killer, so that puts you in front of most of the Craigslist ads I've looked at."

"This is San Francisco; even serial killers need their roommates to stay alive so they can pay the rent. Actually, that would make a great idea for a book," I said.

"A serial killer who becomes great friends with his roommate that he wants to murder but can't because he needs that roommate to stay alive and pay his half of the rent?"

"And slowly, they fall in love."

"Yeah, maybe stick to your day job," Jenny said, laughing.

"You're just saying that because you don't want to have to find another employee," I teased.

"I mean, okay, that's part of it. I've never trained anyone before. I've never done half of this stuff. It looked so easy when Elana did it."

"That's because Elana did most of it badly and only put half the effort into it. You've trained lots of people. You trained me."

"I did not. I showed you how the point-of-sale worked."

"That's literally the definition of training."

"There's so much more to it than that. There's learning how to make the donuts. How to work the coffee machine. Where everything is."

"Yeah, all stuff that you've been doing for years. And teaching people how to do."

"Okay. It's still… I don't know. It feels different now that I'm in charge. I'm really worried I'm going to screw this up. I've got an opportunity here, the chance to do something I've always wanted to do, and I'm so worried about it."

"That's because you care."

"I do. I really do, Poppy. I care so much. I didn't know I would. I wanted to manage this place, but now that I own it, I understand when people say their businesses are their babies. This place looks exactly like I've always wanted it to. I want people to come in here and have the best experience ever. I want people to bring a book and sit by the window and read. I want them to come on their first date here and then come back a year later to propose. I want this to be a place where locals feel a sense of relief when they walk through the doors. And I'm so scared that I'm going to mess it up."

"You won't," I said firmly. "You've been training for this for years, really, even though you don't realize it. I'm not saying everything will be perfect. It won't be. I've learned the hard way that living your dreams isn't a smooth line upwards. But it will be worth it. I do believe that."

"I hope you're right."

"I *know* I'm right. If there's anyone in the world who can make this work, it's you."

"Thanks, Poppy. Also, I'm totally going to take you up on that roommate offer. What happened between you and Juliette?"

"It turns out I'm not cool enough to hang out with her anymore," I replied with a shrug. "It's fine. I was hurt, but I'd rather find out that was the kind of person she was than keep being friends with her for decades without having a clue."

"I'm sorry. It's rough losing a friend."

"It is, but in the long run, I'm better off. I don't want to know someone like her, and I'd much rather be roommates with you. You probably won't try to murder me."

"Not when you're as good at customer service as

Read Between the Lies

you are," Jenny replied with a wink. "When can I move in?"

"Literally whenever. I'll get you a key tomorrow if that works for you?"

"Great, thanks. Mom is going to be happy too. She's been trying to nudge me out the door for almost a year now. I kept telling her I couldn't afford it, and she couldn't complain much, since it was her sister who was paying me minimum wage. Now the pressure is on even more, but at least I've given myself a raise. I just hope I did the math right. I raised the price of donuts by twenty cents, which should more than cover the extra salaries."

"This place looks like the donuts are worth more than twenty cents extra, anyway. Seriously, it looks like you just picked up a bakery from Paris and plonked it right down in the middle of town. The food-court vibes this place used to have are gone. Elana made great donuts, which is what kept this place going, because the marketing and style here were all wrong. They were way too impersonal."

"I'm so glad you see it this way."

"Okay, I have to go. I have a book to write, after all. I'll bring you the keys to my place tomorrow, and you can move in whenever works."

"You're amazing. I'm so glad this has worked out. Here we are, two women in San Francisco, making our own way."

I smiled. "We're going to make it, Jenny. We really are."

Jenny gave me a hug—slightly awkward when I had one arm in a sling, but we made it work—and I said goodbye to her and left. As I was walking back up toward home, I got a text from Ophelia.

I know who the killer is. Call me.

My heart raced as I dialed her number.

Chapter 16

As soon as Ophelia answered, she launched into the whole story. By the time she was finished, I knew she was right.

"So, how are we going to prove it?" I asked.

"That's the tricky part, isn't it? We'll have to come up with a plan."

"Why don't we use me as bait?"

A moment of silence followed on the other end of the line. "Would you be up for that?"

"I wouldn't mind a matching scar on my other shoulder."

"You make a quip like that, but you must realize there's a very real possibility of you getting hurt. And you're already injured."

"I do. But it's the easiest way to draw the killer in, isn't it?"

"Yes. And you will be seen as the limping antelope in a herd full of healthy ones. You would be the most likely to be picked off by our lion."

"There's the animal analogy. You must be confident."

"I am. Are you?"

"Yes. I want to do this. I know it's going to be dangerous. But Ellie stuck her neck out for me. She took a chance on me. She was willing to help me achieve my dreams, and hers were snatched away. I want to see her get justice. I *need* to do this for her."

"Okay. I'll set it up and let you know the details tonight."

"See you then."

My stomach churned as I ended the call. Things were coming to a head. Ophelia had solved the case; we knew who had killed Ellie. And hopefully tomorrow we'd be able to prove it. But for now, I had to put the case out of my head. There was nothing more to be done about it at the moment. Tonight, we were going to steal back a stolen painting, and right now, I was going to continue writing my book.

I headed home, grabbed my laptop from upstairs, and went down to LBB Café. It was the middle of the afternoon rush, so I simply ordered my coffee and a plate of beignets, gratefully found my normal table in the corner in front of the window free, and sat down to work.

Instead of getting the words down on the page

immediately, I started on the framework of the story. I built out the plot: the pinch points, the conflicts between the main characters. The internal and external forces that were keeping them apart. These were the bones of my story, the main structure that would hold it upright. I had to nail this part, because only once my skeleton was strong and standing upright could I take the next step and add the elements that would take it from a bare-bones story to a gorgeous model strutting down the runway that was the front table at my local bookshop.

I spent an hour getting lost in my writing. Occasionally, I'd look up and eat a beignet while watching people filing past the coffee shop. At one point, my phone binged. It was a text from Lily behind the counter. It was a GIF of a cat at a laptop, dressed in a onesie, typing at warp speed.

I laughed to myself, sent a couple of emojis in reply, then went back to my work. After a couple of hours, I had the barest structure figured out. I probably should have done this before I'd actually written the first fifteen percent of the book, but life was about learning. And I was learning to write a book. My foundation was solid, and I would be able to build around it now.

I wanted Amanda's journey to be as much about accepting herself internally as it was about falling in love with Devon. This was going to be a story about a woman falling in love with a man, yes, but it would also be about a woman falling in love with herself.

I was fiddling with one of the conflict points when suddenly, Lily slipped into the seat across from me.

"It's nice to see you hard at work. You're concentrating."

"I really need this, Lily. I need it to be good."

"It will be."

"I'm glad you have faith in me, at least."

"I do, and I also want your opinion on something. It's finally quietened down a bit. How would you like a whole bunch of free coffee? I know it's four in the afternoon, and this is probably a bad idea, but we just got a whole bunch of new blends in from the roaster, and I need someone who isn't Laura Belle or John to try them out."

"Why have they refused?" I asked with a grin.

"Well, John doesn't drink coffee."

"Really? But he's such a good barista."

"I know. It's a mystery to me too. He says that because he doesn't drink it, it means he has to understand the methodology and science behind the coffee, since he can't go by taste alone. I think that's just him bullshitting and being pretentious, but what do I know? He makes great coffee, so I can't complain."

"And Laura Belle?"

"She's been out the back all day singing along to the new Carly Rae Jepsen album, and I'm this close to slipping her a Valium and telling customers we don't have any more baked goods today. The last thing I'm giving that woman is caffeine for *more* energy."

I laughed. "Okay, fair enough. Sure, I'll help out."

"You're the best, Poppy, thank you. Of course, you don't have to try them all."

"Funnily enough, tonight is actually a great time for it. I'll have to stay awake half the night. I was going to try and have a nap, but it's still going to be a long one, and I'm not eighteen anymore."

"Okay, well, how about this? I'll make you some iced coffees, and you can take them upstairs with you and try them at your leisure."

"Sure. But full disclosure, I don't exactly have a refined palate. I won't be able to tell you that this coffee has berry undertones, or that that one has a hint of caramel aftertaste. But I know if I like a coffee and if I don't."

"That's all I need, really. A comparison to our current blend could be good too."

"No problem. I didn't realize you change the beans from time to time."

"We keep the same blend running through the machine in here a lot of the time. After all, it's a good blend, and our regulars like it. But at the same time, I know there can be room for improvement, and I'm always willing to try some new flavors from our roasters. Even if we don't change our basic blend that runs through the machine, we also sell a few different flavors of whole roasted beans, and I like to rotate those a couple of times a year."

"In that case, by all means, I am willing to try as much coffee as you're willing to give me," I said with a grin.

"Great," Lily said, rapping her knuckles on the table as she got up. "Just promise me if you're going to start singing that you've got a better voice than Laura Belle. I love her, but her singing voice sounds like two racoons in a back alley who are either fighting or banging, and they're too into it for you to want to check which one it is."

I laughed. "Thanks for that visual."

"You're very welcome. You should include it in your book. It's very romantic."

"No kidding."

Lily shot me a wink then headed back behind the counter. This had worked out well. I could totally use a large supply of free coffee for tonight; I was going to need it.

I grabbed a beignet and bit into the soft dough, getting back to my outline. About ten minutes later, Lily dropped off a tray full of iced coffee in take-out cups, and I shot her a grateful smile. "This is going to be perfect for the big night I have ahead of me. Thank you."

She wiggled her eyebrows. "Anything to do with that guy you were in here with a few days ago?"

"No," I replied quickly, my face quickly going

cherry red. Great. This was all I needed. To be almost thirty and still blushing like a teenager at the mere mention of dating a guy. Thanks, body. "It's, uh, something different. Something with Ophelia, my new friend."

"Oh, fun."

"And I don't think I told you, but tomorrow I'm starting work at STD again. Only the name has changed, and Elana sold the business to her niece, Jenny."

"Thank goodness for that."

"I think we're all glad that name has finally been given some antibiotics and is well and truly dead," I said, chuckling.

"What is it called now? I'm almost afraid to ask."

"La Bonne Bouche. I don't know what it means, though it's obviously French. The new style is super cute too. Jenny has done a great job with it. She's nervous, obviously, since she's got a loan now that she has to pay back, but I think if anyone can make it work, it'll be her."

Lily nodded. "Tell her to come here if she needs some advice, or just an ear from another entrepreneur who's made it work. It's not easy, especially when she's just starting out. And Jenny is young, right?"

"Twenty-two, I think, yeah. She is. But she's got a good head on her shoulders."

"She's going to be treating you well? That's the

most important thing for a business owner, is to take care of their staff. You can't take care of the customers until your staff is taken care of, first. Do you know John gets ten job offers a month from other cafés in town?"

I raised my eyebrows. "I didn't realize that."

"He placed in last year's national barista championships."

"I also didn't realize that was a thing."

"He's turned down every one, because Laura Belle and I make sure that he's happy here."

"That's fantastic. I'll introduce you to Jenny. She's going to move in with me, too, since I need to replace Juliette's spot as a roommate. She wants to be closer to the shop than Oakland, so I'm sure you'll get to know her."

"I look forward to meeting her. There's a customer, so I have to go."

Lily headed back to the counter, and I finished off my coffee, eyeing the others. Then I checked my watch. The greedy part of me wanted to enjoy one now, but I also knew it would be smarter to keep them until later. After all, I wanted to make good life choices, and if I was going to be stealing a fifty-million-dollar Kandinsky painting tonight, I needed to take a nap first.

I packed up my computer, thanked Lily again, promised to have my review in by tomorrow—assuming we didn't get caught—then headed upstairs. I had a big night ahead of me.

Chapter 17

I HAD ALWAYS PRIDED MYSELF ON BEING THE KIND of person who could sleep through anything. Fire alarm? Check. The middle seat of a Spirit Airlines flight? Check. I was basically a koala with opposable thumbs. But tonight, with the looming prospect of committing grand theft, returning a priceless piece of art to a museum, and ideally not getting caught in the process, the nap that usually came so easily evaded me. I rolled around, tossing and turning on my single mattress in the corner of the living room, trying to get comfortable, closing my eyes, counting sheep, doing everything I could.

But no matter what I did, sleep wouldn't come. Every time I closed my eyes, I thought about tonight. What if something went wrong? What if we were caught? What if I'd narrowly evaded arrest for murder, and two weeks later found myself in jail for a crime that this time, I did commit?

I'd never done anything like this before in my life. I'd grown up being a good girl, in every way. I obeyed the rules. I kept my head down, worked hard, and did what I was supposed to. And now? Now, I found myself agreeing to take part in an art heist. Sure, it was for a good cause, but the law didn't distinguish between crimes that were done for good and crimes that were done for evil.

Unless you're Batman. And I wasn't Batman.

When I thought back to even two weeks ago, my life was completely different. It was wild how quickly things could change. And yet, there was no part of me that thought I should renege on this plan. No warning lights going off in my brain, telling me to call Ophelia and tell her that I was sorry but needed to back out.

This was what I wanted to do, because it was right. Kyle Wellman had stolen—or purchased a stolen—Kandinsky. He knew what it was. He displayed it in his office as a show of arrogance, and he didn't deserve to have it. It belonged in a museum, and I was going to make sure it went back there.

But it would be really nice if I could get a bit of sleep first.

After ninety minutes of tossing and turning, I gave up. The adrenaline was winning, and there was no way I was going to get that nap in. Instead, I headed to the fridge and pried one of the iced coffees free from the tray Lily had given me. I swirled it around a little bit then took a sip.

Right away, my taste buds lit up, in a "this doesn't taste like the coffee you usually drink" kind of way. This one tasted… Well, I'd already gone on record to say that my actual perception of tastes wasn't the greatest. But it was a richer flavor than the regular blend, like someone had taken it and twisted the flavor dial up to 11.

Lily had written letters on the top of each. This one was "B", so I pulled out my phone and sent her a text. *I'm a big fan of B so far. Top-tier.*

She sent back a GIF of SpongeBob and Patrick celebrating.

I grabbed a second coffee and had a sip of that one as well. Not nearly as good. When I sent my report on that one through, Lily replied with a GIF of sad Pikachu.

I'll get to the other two after I come back. But yeah, that first one is a winner. You need to consider making it your normal bean, because no offense, but I like it more than the one you're using now.

That good, you think?

Yeah. Didn't you try them?

Sure. But I don't want to give you my opinion until you've tried them.

Okay. I'll come in tomorrow after work with my final consensus.

Lily sent over a GIF of a sign reading "you're the

best" while colorful fireworks exploded in the background. I smiled and swiped back to the home screen. My eyes moved upward to check the time; there were still three hours to go before I had to meet Ophelia.

I pulled my laptop toward me and started writing.

At ten thirty, I got ready to go. I dressed in all black then threw a white sweater over the top to make myself look less suspicious before splurging on an Uber to take me downtown. With no traffic, the ride took only a shade over five minutes, and before I knew it, I was heading up to her office, my heart pounding.

I was pretty sure this was the first real crime I'd ever committed. Not counting speeding, underage drinking, or smoking a little bit of weed here and there before it was legalized. No, this was *crime* crime. It wasn't until the elevator was well and truly whisking me upwards that the implications of getting caught really hit me. I could go to jail.

On the bright side, assuming we didn't use any weapons tonight, we'd only be on the hook for grand theft if we were caught. In California, that was theft with a value of over $950. Which yeah, a fifty-million-dollar painting definitely qualified, but the penalty didn't go up the higher the value of the painting you stole.

The maximum punishment was three years in jail, a ten-thousand-dollar fine, and definitely being completely disowned by my family. Okay, that third one might be more of a blessing than a punishment. But still, I wasn't a big fan of those first two.

The door opened with a light rattle, and I stepped out into Ophelia's office as if my legs worked on autopilot, putting one foot in front of the other while my brain screamed that this was a bad idea. And you know what? It was. I knew that. But it was also the right thing to do. That painting didn't rightfully belong to Kyle Wellman. It belonged to a museum. And we were going to bring it back there.

"Welcome," Ophelia said when I reached the conference room. Sameen was already there, wearing a beautiful deep green suit with a pale pink blouse, her dark hair cascading down her shoulders. Even now she was dressed like a professional. Next to her was Fiona in jeans and a plain black T-shirt with some flat white sandals, the most casual attire I'd seen her wear so far.

Sitting next to Ophelia was another woman, leaning casually back in her chair. Dressed in a navy blue jumpsuit with camel-colored ankle boots, one of which rested on her knee, her chocolate brown hair had just the slightest copper shimmer to it. Her large, rounded deep brown eyes were heavily made up and expressive, almost to the point of being mesmerizing, and her mouth curled upward into a cheeky smile, the bold red color standing out against her tawny skin.

"Poppy, meet Taylor," Ophelia said with a smile. Tonight, she was dressed in black leggings and sneakers and a tight-fitting, long-sleeved black top. I was glad to see it; we were dressed pretty much identically.

"Hi," I said to her with a smile.

She gave me a slow nod in response. Her smile didn't change one bit, which was just a little unsettling.

"All right," Ophelia said, clapping her hands together. "We're all here, so let's get organized. Tonight, we steal back a painting that was taken from its rightful place at a museum in Lisbon seventeen years ago. Sameen, you're on deck in case anything goes wrong and we need to find ourselves bailed out of jail."

"I'll be here, both presuming and hoping that my services will not be required tonight."

"Fiona, you know the drill."

"I'm on the computer, listening to the police scanner, trying to intercept any kind of communication that might indicate we've been reported, and watching the nearby CCTV footage. I'll get started now. When will you be in position?"

"Within forty minutes."

"I'll be ready. Good luck, ladies."

Fiona got up and strode down the hall to her office.

"I'm going to get ready for court tomorrow while I wait to see if you're both involved too. It's that other case. Daniel Grower," she said to Fiona. "Pre-trial hearings."

"Good. Keep me up-to-date on that one, will you?"

"Sure thing." Sameen flashed me a smile, nodded to Taylor, then left the room.

Taylor looked at me. "You're Ophelia's second on this? I trust her, but I gotta be blunt: you look like you're about to shit your pants. And you've got one functional arm. Don't tell me you're going to bail on this. A setup like this, no one is allowed to bail."

"I'm fine," I said, hoping my voice held on better than my nerves did. Luckily, the voice that came out was strong and confident.

"Good," Taylor replied. "This your first job?"

"Yes."

"You never forget your first," she said with a smile. "Especially when you've only got one useful arm."

"I'll be fine," I replied coolly. I had the distinct feeling Taylor was testing me. "Why are you here?"

"I'm the getaway driver," Taylor said with a wink. "I'm the fastest gas pedal in the west."

"And the most subtle," Ophelia said. "Don't forget that part. It's one thing to win a race against the police, but it's even better to not end up in one in the first place."

"It's much less fun, though."

I was starting to understand why Fiona had referred to her as a psychopath earlier today. "So, how do the two of you know each other? Going by your accent, you're American?" I asked Taylor.

"Yes. Born and raised in LA. About ten years ago, I was in... where was it, Budapest? Three in the morning, just going for a nice evening drive. I turn the corner and find Ophelia being chased by three men who obviously didn't have the best intentions."

"So you stopped and picked her up?"

"Sure did. After I hit two of them with my car. Got the third one when I reversed."

"They were members of a gang I was trying to take down at the time," Ophelia said, a nostalgic smile crossing her face. "I'd made a mistake and had gotten caught. It was just after Fiona left, and the replacement I'd found wasn't quite as skilled as she was. Luckily, Taylor was there to save the day."

"What happened to the gang?"

"I'd collected enough proof of what they were doing that I went to visit the leader in the hospital."

"I broke his femur," Taylor announced proudly.

"He saw what I had, and while he did try to kill me, I had a definite advantage. I was able to convince him that it was in his best interest to get out of town and leave his client alone, lest he spend the last half of his life in prison, and he believed me."

"It was basically a fairy tale, complete with happily ever after."

"I'm not sure a lot of fairy tales involve running people over with a car," I pointed out.

"They should," Taylor said with a grin. "It's so much more interesting than a glass slipper. What's the situation tonight, Ophelia?"

"You're not going to like it. No Maserati for you, Taylor. Not even my Audi. Because the painting is big, we're going in a plain white van."

"Always a classic. A classic that's not a great getaway vehicle."

"Well, with Fiona back on board, we shouldn't need it. I trust her. If the police decide to come break up the party, we'll be long gone."

"I hope so," I said. "I didn't duck a murder charge just to get nailed for a robbery I actually did commit."

"Don't worry. I haven't been arrested yet, and I don't intend to break that streak tonight."

"I can't decide if I'm more worried or relieved about the fact that this apparently isn't your first major theft," I said.

"Oh, you should definitely be more relieved. Now, let's go over the plan. This should be a quick in-and-out, but we're unsure about the security situation. I think he's going to try to be subtle about it. Kyle Wellman isn't going to want to draw much attention to the painting, so he won't go all-out trying to protect it. The plan as it stands is this: we drive down, and Taylor drops us off four blocks away. We walk the rest of the way and do a visual check. Fiona should have eyes on the door thanks to a camera on the building across the street, but we still want to do an in-person check. Then we go in. We get the painting. Taylor meets us outside, and we get out. We reconvene back here, painting in tow."

"When you put it that way, it almost sounds easy," Taylor said. "I guess this means I don't get to have any fun?"

"Not if we do things right."

"I hate how competent you are."

"You don't want to have to outrun anyone in a plain white van, anyway. I don't want to draw suspicion to us, so it's got an ordinary engine."

"Boring."

"My apologies. I'll do my best next time to ensure our criminal enterprise also entertains you."

"I'd appreciate it. And make it something with a flashier car. I haven't driven a Lambo in a while. I will admit they're terrible getaway vehicles, though."

"Because they stand out?" I asked.

"Yup. Did you ever play *Grand Theft Auto* as a kid?" I shook my head, and Taylor continued. "When you committed a crime near the cops and they came after you, the easiest way to get them off your tail was to go into a body shop and get your car painted, because they couldn't recognize you. Real life is the same way. You don't want to

Read Between the Lies

do anything illegal in a car that's going to attract attention. Here's some good life advice: commit all your crimes in a five-year-old Camry. It'll look like any other old car. Half the population can't even properly identify it. They'll tell the cops it was a Corolla, or a Civic. But you rob a jewelry store in a Ferrari, and people will *know*. They'll recognize the car, because even somewhere like San Francisco, where the rich and famous spend their money on fancy cars to show off how big their dicks—I mean, their bank accounts are, there aren't so many around that it doesn't catch your eye when you see one of those beasts driving past."

"I'll keep that in mind. Personally, I'm hoping this is the last crime I commit, ever."

Taylor laughed, the sound ringing through the office. "Around Ophelia? Please."

"She doesn't strike me as the kind of person to commit crimes for fun."

"For fun? No, absolutely not. That's more my jam. But for justice? Yes, Ophelia will do anything she has to do to solve a case. And she brought you in on this for a reason. She thinks you're one of us."

"And who is that, exactly?"

"The people in this world who aren't happy living normal lives. The people who need more. Who want more. Whatever that might be. I need the adrenaline. I can't live without it. It's my drug, and you can't just inject it into my veins. Ophelia needs the puzzle. She needs to exercise her brain and solve the problems no one else can."

"And what about Fiona?" I asked, turning to Ophelia.

"Fiona needs information. That's how she's always been. She wants to know everything, at all times, and the internet is such a great way for her to get it," Taylor said. Then she asked, "What about you? What brings you here? What do you need, more than anything in the world?"

"To prove myself," I found myself answering, without even thinking about the question. And as the words came out of my mouth, I knew they were true.

"That's a start. How did you hurt your arm?"

"Got stabbed saving Ophelia from a murderer."

Taylor raised an eyebrow slightly, as if I'd just told her the local bookstore was closing an hour early. I had a feeling she was a hard woman to surprise. "I suppose I should thank you. Life is much more interesting when you know Ophelia."

"As much as you're thanking me, I'm even more grateful for her. She saved my life first, in a way."

"Still, if it comes down to it, are you willing to use that other arm? You never know what's going to happen in a situation like this."

"If it stops me from spending three years in jail, I will literally hack it off myself."

"That's a bit of an overreaction. It's only three

years. I'd lose a finger for that, but a whole arm? To each their own, I guess."

"I wasn't aware we were negotiating body parts for prison time."

"You started it."

"It was an example."

To my surprise, Taylor grinned. "I like you. You've got spunk. Most people are too scared of me right off the bat to try to argue with me."

"Should I be scared of you?"

"Terrified."

"I'll just try to stay away from your cars, since you seem prone to running people over with them."

"Only when they deserve it," she said with a wink.

"All right, ladies," Ophelia said. "If you're ready, I think we're going to get going."

It was time to commit my first-ever felony.

Chapter 18

SAMEEN WAS TYPING AWAY AT HER COMPUTER AS we walked past, and Fiona waved us in as we passed her office.

"I've got eyes on the door and your drop-off spot four blocks away. Both look clear from here, but as always, be careful."

"We will. You have your headset?"

"Yes."

"Good. Make the group call when I send you a text."

"Will do. Good luck."

Ophelia nodded, and the three of us headed down to the street. About half a block from the office was the aforementioned plain white van. All it was missing to look incredibly creepy was Free Candy spray-painted onto the side. Ophelia tossed a set of keys to Taylor, who caught them with one hand.

"We're riding in the back," Ophelia told me. She pulled the van's sliding door open, the screech giving away the fact that the rails could have used a good dose of WD-40. Then she grabbed a wig from the floor and tossed it onto the driver's seat. "That's for you," she called out to Taylor when she opened the door.

"I always thought I'd make a hot blonde," Taylor replied with a grin.

"In case we get caught on security tapes?" I asked as I climbed into the back of the van with Ophelia.

"Yes. I'm a strong proponent of covering every possibility. You can never be too careful when committing a crime. One of the most common mistakes people make is not factoring in the arrival and the escape. They factor in everything that can happen when they're in the middle of it, but they don't think about the other things. I don't want us to be caught on camera and have Taylor identified. You're probably nervous, but don't worry. I do things right."

"It's weird to say, but of everyone I know, I think you're the one I trust the most to pull off a heist like this."

Ophelia shot me a smile. "Thank you."

"Let's get ready to rumble, ladies!" Taylor called out from the driver's seat, and a moment later, the key turned in the ignition and the engine struggled to life. It caught after turning over a couple of times, though, and Taylor pulled away from the curb and headed toward the warehouse.

There were no seats in the back of the van, so we sat on the floor while Taylor drove. She was obviously obeying every law; the occasional sound of the blinker broke the silence. My throat was dry, and the closer we got, the more real it felt.

Ophelia reached across the van and handed me an earpiece. "Put this in and tap the button on the outside when it rings," she ordered. I did as she said. Taylor automatically held a hand out behind her, and Ophelia put one in hers as well.

Twenty seconds later, I heard the familiar sound of a phone ringing, and I tapped the outside of the earpiece.

"Hello?"

"This is Mission Control," I heard Fiona's voice say on the other end.

"Just like the old days," Ophelia said.

"In the old days, my husband didn't think I was meeting an old college friend for drinks," Fiona replied.

"As long as you're here," Taylor said. "I've heard a lot about your skills, and I'm interested in seeing them in action."

"What's your ETA?" Fiona asked.

"Two minutes out."

"Cameras are clear. Hopefully we'll get it on the first try."

"We will," Ophelia said confidently. "Have we met?"

"Aren't there two doors that potentially have that painting?"

"In theory, yes. But in practice, I'll be able to get it on the first try."

"How?" I asked.

"Oh, that's Ophelia," Taylor said. "None of us know how she does it, but she will. If she says she knows, she knows. Anyway, here we are."

"I'll let you know what building we're in when we get there. Be ready. I plan on being quick."

"I'll be faster than the guy I met at an Oscars after-party a couple years ago who swore he would rock my world."

"Well, I'll never be able to unhear that comparison."

"You think that's bad? Try watching movies where he's the main love interest," Taylor said as she pulled the van over and slowed to a stop. "Good luck."

"Ready?" Ophelia asked me.

"As I'll ever be."

Ophelia nodded and pulled the van door open, the sound seeming louder, like a rumbling train. I jumped out, and gravel crunched beneath my feet. Ophelia followed immediately after me and closed the door behind her.

"Let's go."

Taylor cut the engine, and the lights immediately went out. I could barely make out Ophelia in front of me as my eyes adjusted to the light. There were no twinkles from the stars above; it was cloudy out, which also blocked any light the moon might have offered. This was good; while I struggled to get used to the low light, it also meant the odds of being spotted were lower too.

Luckily, this place didn't seem like a high-risk area. Every few seconds, the sound of a car on the freeway up above cut through, but there was no way any of the drivers would be able to spot us down below. Other than that, there was only silence. This was an industrial part of town; most of the happenings here were during business hours. The middle of the night was for sketchy stuff only.

Like what we were doing.

Ophelia obviously knew the way. I tried to take deep breaths, easing the pounding in my chest as my heart put on a performance that would have made Phil Collins proud. It was going to be fine. We walked in silence, against the sides of buildings where possible, keeping as far into the shadows as possible. When we had to cross the street, we checked to make sure the coast was clear then darted across.

I'd never felt more like a raccoon in my life.

Before I knew it, we were right where Fiona had shown us on Google Street View. The buildings were darker and more imposing now, of course, what with it being the middle of the night, but I recognized the buildings with the two different entrances.

"So, how will you know which one of these houses the painting?" I whispered.

"Come and look," Ophelia said, motioning for me to follow her. We headed to the brown building, where the old-style doors were on rails.

"I have eyes on you," Fiona said through the headset. "Don't worry. I'm duplicating blank footage and altering the time-stamp as we go; anyone from the security company watching this won't see anything."

We weren't actually committing any crimes yet —nothing said you couldn't be outdoors, dressed in black in the middle of the night—and yet the knowledge that we were on camera right now still sent a jolt of adrenaline through me.

Ophelia pulled out a pen light and shone it on the rails. "Here," she whispered. "This one has been opened recently. The rail is slightly shiny. Do you see that?"

"Yeah."

"If this warehouse was abandoned, the metal rails would be dull."

"So it's this one?"

"It might be. We have to go and check out the other doors first."

Ophelia and I crossed the street to the other warehouse building. Ophelia went to the first roller door. "This one isn't it."

"How do you know?"

"Look at the seal, where the roller door meets the ground. It's full of dirt, grease, and gunk. No, this door hasn't been opened in quite some time."

We rushed over to the next one, where there was a definite break in the seal of dirt at the bottom. "It could be this one too. We've narrowed it down to two places, at least. Let's try this one first."

Next to the roller doors in this building were stairs that led to a regular-sized door. Ophelia raced up them, pulled a small box of tools from her bag, and got to work. Within seconds, I heard the lock turn in the door, and she opened it.

"We're in," she announced. "Fiona, do you know if there's a security system in here?"

"I can't find one if there is. But keep an eye out for a flashing light somewhere, just in case. Does this one have the painting?"

"Uncertain," Ophelia replied. She pulled out her phone and turned on the light, and I did the same. This warehouse was almost empty. There were about twenty random boxes scattered around the place, but nothing else. I looked around, but I couldn't see any sign of a security system that needed to be disarmed.

"None of these boxes look like they're big enough for that painting," I said, stepping to the box closest to me. It wasn't sealed, so I pulled back the cardboard, reached in, and pulled out a vacuum-sealed bag. In it was a piece of cloth, and when I looked closely at it, I realized what it was.

"Is this... underwear?" I asked Ophelia, squinting at the fabric. It certainly was. On the other side of the vacuum bag was a label describing the item:

- Size: small
- Length of wear: 48h
- Color: black
- Special request: worn to the gym

Shocked, I dropped the pair of underwear back into the box, but curiosity got the better of me, and I grabbed another pair. This one was medium sized, and when I looked at the special requests, I started laughing.

"What is it?"

"This one has been peed in. I don't think the Kandinsky painting is in here, unless Kyle Wellman is into panty sniffing. I think we've uncovered someone's panty-selling operation. Probably on the internet."

"It certainly appears that way," Ophelia said with a chuckle. "There are a lot here. It must be a group."

"The internet is the weirdest place. Ew, this one specifically requested panties with skid marks," I said, dropping another bag back into the box. "This is definitely not where the painting is."

Read Between the Lies

"No, but whoever is shipping these panties off to buyers is likely making a very nice profit," Ophelia said.

"Are there really that many buyers for this stuff? I guess so."

"Yes, and some people buy in bulk."

"I like to think I'm not a prude, but who out there is treating their used panty purchases like they're on a trip to Costco?"

Ophelia laughed. "They are out there."

"No kidding. How much would one of these pairs sell for?"

"Beats me," Ophelia said.

"Anywhere from forty to a hundred bucks plus, depending on how weird the request is," Taylor's voice said on the other end of the line.

"Do you have a kink you want to tell us about?" I asked with a grin.

"No, but when I was in college, my funding options were either working as a waitress for tips in exchange for getting my ass grabbed constantly, or selling my panties to weirdos online for a hundred bucks a pop. That was kind of a no-brainer."

"That's actually fascinating," I said.

"The key is to actually deliver. It's like any other business: quality counts. Some people would spit on the underwear to make them extra crusty, but the guys know. I never would. If someone wants to pay me to wear a pair of panties for two days straight, that's what they're going to get. Especially when it's costing them a Benjamin every time."

"How long did you do it?" Fiona asked.

"Who said I stopped?"

"Wait, are you still doing it now?" I said.

Taylor laughed. "No. I did stop, after college. I found other ways to make even more money, which became a better use of my time."

"Where did you sell them?"

"Reddit, mostly."

"Okay, I know this conversation is fascinating, but we have a painting to steal, and it's obviously not here," Ophelia interrupted. "Can we talk about the intricacies of selling used panties on the internet at our celebratory breakfast in a few hours instead?"

"Sorry," I mumbled as I put the panties back and closed the box. Ophelia was right. We carefully made sure everything was how we'd left it, stepped back out into the night, and crossed back to the other warehouse.

Chapter 19

The warehouse that hopefully stored the painting was harder to get into. For one thing, there was no easy exterior door access like there had been with the panty storage unit. The large door was kept shut with a very heavy-duty-looking combination lock.

"Are we just going to smash it?" I asked Ophelia, eyeing the lock carefully. It didn't look like it would be easy to open.

"I much prefer finesse to brute force, where possible," Ophelia replied. She pulled out another tool, which she slid into the lock side of the combination. Within seconds, it was open.

"Wow. That looked too easy."

"I'll let you in on a little secret: people like to believe that combination locks are safe, but they're actually incredibly easy to get into. Your real goal isn't to get a lock that's foolproof, because they don't exist: you just want to make it look like yours is harder to get into than the next one over."

"Good to know," I said as Ophelia motioned for me to help her. I grabbed the door with my free arm, and the two of us pulled on the door as hard as we could. The old, wooden door squealed its displeasure, but it slowly acquiesced, sliding open while sounding like a dying creature in a bad horror movie from the fifties.

When the gap was about two feet wide, Ophelia stepped inside.

"We're in," she said. "But there's a security system. Give me a minute."

Ophelia turned on her phone camera and headed straight for the security system in the corner. The red light blinked ominously, waiting the thirty seconds for us to fail to enter a code.

"What are we going to do? Does Fiona know the code?" I asked quietly.

"Ophelia doesn't need me for this," Fiona replied. "I don't like hacking into security companies if I don't have to when we do things like this; it leaves too much room for being spotted. Better to do it manually."

Ophelia looked at the keypad carefully. "See how four of the numbers are faded? One, three, six and eight? Those are the four numbers used in the code. The three is the most faded of all, which

Read Between the Lies

means it's the first number, as people have the most dirt and grime on their fingers before touching it. The one is the least faded; that means it's our last number. The others are pretty even, but our lizard brains love patterns more than anything, and the six is just above the three. So we're going to try three-six-eight-one."

Ophelia punched that code in order, and a second later, the red flashing light turned green. I let out a breath of relief.

"Done," Ophelia said with satisfaction. "We're in."

"Is the painting there?" Taylor asked.

I turned on my phone camera and looked around. This warehouse was far larger than the other one had been. The walls were made of wood and looked like they could have used a fresh coat of paint about fifty years ago. The concrete floor had a solid layer of dust, and there were a handful of boxes around but not many. Frankly, it looked like no one had been in this warehouse in a decade, except for the one wrapped item pressed up against the back wall.

"I think we have it," Ophelia said as my light shone on what was certainly going to be the Kandinsky painting. I stepped closer to get a better look. It had been enclosed in a wooden frame then covered in about five or six layers of bubble wrap and more plastic than an episode of *Dexter*.

"This was done by a professional," I pointed out.

"I would certainly hope so."

"Do we assume it's the painting, or are we actually going to look at it?"

"My father liked to say, when you assume, you make an 'ass' out of 'u' and 'me.' I always hated that saying. There are times when it's better to assume, and I think this is one of them. Taylor, how quickly can you have the van here? I believe we have our painting."

"Thirty seconds," Taylor replied. Ophelia motioned for me to go to the other side of the painting, and the two of us carried it to the door. I was surprised by how light the canvas was. I guess I had expected that a multi-million-dollar painting would weigh more than just a few pounds, but even with just the one arm, I was able to lift it easily in its wooden frame.

We reached the door and stood in the shadows. I kept an ear out, and ten seconds later, heard the low rumble of the engine. Taylor pulled up in front of the door, raced out of the vehicle, and opened the back doors of the van. The three of us got the painting in.

"Get in," Ophelia ordered. She raced back to the warehouse door, went inside for 10 seconds— presumably to reset the security system—came out, pushed the heavy door closed, and locked it again.

Then she jumped into the van after us, pulling the door closed. Taylor immediately pulled out, did a U-turn, and began to drive.

It wasn't until we were a couple of blocks away that I realized just how much this had affected me. My heart was pounding. I was breathing heavily, and a thin sheen of sweat covered my skin. We had just done it! We'd stolen a fifty-million-dollar painting.

"What happens now? We take it back to the office?"

"That is the plan. I will alert Jean-Paul, and he will organize a team to collect the painting and take it back to Europe, where it will be returned to its rightful owner."

"Don't you risk getting arrested if you do that?"

"Oh, technically, yes. But in practice, Jean-Paul knows much better than to try it. Besides, he'll be thrilled that he actually has the painting to return to his boss."

"Not that I want to alarm anybody, but I think we've got a tail," Taylor said. "Black SUV, been behind me for a couple of minutes. It's definitely not a cop."

The van having no windows, there was no way for me to have a look out at who was following us. Taylor, to her credit, simply accelerated slowly. Suddenly, three quick pops hit the door at the back of the van.

"Are you seriously shooting at a metal door? Morons. At least go for the tires," Taylor muttered. "All right, ladies. Hold on, this ride is about to get interesting."

"They have guns?" I asked Ophelia, my mouth going dry.

"Don't worry. Taylor knows what she's doing."

I certainly hoped so.

"Should I… I don't know, duck or something? I don't have a lot of experience getting shot at."

"The van will take care of it," Ophelia said as she heard another pop. "Taylor is right; they're not shooting at the tires, which would have been far more intelligent, so we're not dealing with the brightest bulbs this morning. It will be fine."

I closed my eyes and tried not to think too hard about what was going on as the van lurched to the left. It picked up speed; Taylor must have merged onto the highway.

"Must be nice to have spent all that money on that SUV, only to have no idea how to drive it," Taylor muttered from the front seat. The shooting stopped; the drivers must not have wanted to attract that much attention to themselves.

"We're safe on the highway," Ophelia said, mirroring my thoughts. "Above all, Kyle Wellman wants discretion. He knows that if we're caught, if we're seen here, that his possession of the Kandinsky is lost."

The van swerved from side to side, and I resisted

the urge to vomit. Whether that urge came from the movement of the vehicle or the whole situation I currently found myself in, I had no idea. Next thing I knew, though, the van swerved so quickly to the left I was pretty sure two of the wheels actually came off the ground, and a second later, Taylor let out a whoop of satisfaction.

"There's nothing quite like a last-second swerve onto an exit ramp to lose people," she announced. "Ladies, we're home free."

I'd never been happier to hear those words in my life.

About ten minutes later, the van slowed to a stop. The three of us jumped right back into action, with Ophelia and me carrying the painting into the lobby of her building. It wouldn't fit in the small elevator, so we slowly took the stairs up to the third floor.

"Are we just going to leave it in your office? Can't anyone get in?"

"I can actually lock the elevator so that the third floor can only be accessed with a key card," Ophelia explained. "And the door via the stairwell is locked as well."

"If I've learned anything today, it's that locks are basically toys for toddlers."

Ophelia chuckled. "True, but mine are a little bit more heavy-duty than most. I trust that the painting will be safe in the office. Besides, it's not like we'll leave it out in the open. We'll hide it.

Wellman is going to be made aware that the painting was taken, and I imagine it won't be difficult for him to find out who has it. Fiona, we're just about at the door, if you can open it for us."

About thirty seconds later, we reached the top of the stairs, where Fiona had the door propped open. We stepped inside, and Ophelia motioned for me to follow her into the big conference room. Fiona took over carrying Ophelia's end of the painting while Ophelia headed to the conference table. She reached underneath it, and a moment later, I gasped as the large wall to the side, where images were projected onto, shifted about a foot, revealing a secret room behind it.

"Sometimes I swear it's like you're literally living in a movie," I said as Fiona and I entered the empty room—it was plain, with white walls, and completely empty. Then we leaned the painting against a wall and emerged from it. Ophelia tapped under the table once more, and the wall moved back into place, as if we'd never been there at all.

"That room has been quite useful a few times," she said. "Now, come on. Let's all go get an early breakfast and celebrate our achievement tonight."

Ophelia pulled the speaker from her ear then dropped it on the floor and crushed it beneath her foot. Fiona and I did the same, and shortly thereafter, Sameen joined us.

"Congratulations on another well-executed plan," she said, shaking Ophelia's hand. "I'm always

Read Between the Lies

happy when your late-night excursions don't cause more work for me."

"Glad to be of service," Ophelia replied. "Taylor should be back soon."

"She's getting rid of the van?" I asked.

"Yes. The license plates will be untraceable, but all the same, I need them to disappear. She knows the drill. We'll meet her at the diner."

"You're nothing if not a creature of habit," Fiona said then turned to me. "When we lived in London, Ophelia always wanted to go to the worst place in the world after our completely middle-of-the-night missions. It was this terrible diner in central London that made Waffle House look like a Michelin-star restaurant."

Ophelia laughed. "You're such a snob. The food wasn't great, but it was open twenty-four seven."

"Until the health inspectors finally shut it down permanently last year. Did you know I kept an eye on its ratings? It had a 2.4-star average at the end. Do you know how bad a restaurant has to be to get an average that low? The world's worst McDonald's has a higher rating than that."

"Well, I promise you, the place we're going now will suit your high standards. You *are* coming, aren't you? I will admit, I'll be very disappointed if you bail on us now."

Fiona sighed. "Daniel and the kids are certainly asleep by now, anyway. What's another hour? Yes, I'll come."

"So pleased to hear it."

The four of us—Ophelia, Fiona, Sameen, and I —piled into the elevator and headed down to the lobby.

We'd successfully stolen a fifty-million-dollar Kandinsky.

Chapter 20

THE PINECREST DINER WAS ONLY A FEW BLOCKS away from Ophelia's office, at the far end of Union Square, where it bordered the Tenderloin. Located in an unassuming corner building next to the ornate American Conservatory Theatre, a sign above the diner advertised that it was open twenty-four hours, and the place was bustling for just after two in the morning.

Taylor waved at us from one of the booths when we entered, and soon enough the five of us perused the expansive menus. I tried to decide if it was late enough for a burger or early enough for breakfast.

"Van is taken care of?" Ophelia asked as we slid into the booth.

"Sure is. They'll never find it. The painting?"

"Stored and secure."

The server arrived then to take our drink orders, and we all ordered copious amounts of coffee—

Taylor's exact order was "if you've got an IV to plug it directly into my veins, that would be great"—and the five of us settled in to chat as we browsed the menus.

"I can't believe you used to sell panties on the internet," Fiona said to Taylor in a quiet voice.

"You obviously haven't met Taylor if you're actually surprised by that," Sameen said with a laugh.

Taylor shrugged. "It was easy money. Honestly, the most annoying part was the ability to scale. It's not like I can grow a second coochie to wear more panties every day."

I choked on my own saliva and quickly brought my menu to my face.

"Prude," Taylor said to me as the waitress returned with our coffee.

We placed our orders then continued to chat. "The thing is, it was basically sex-work adjacent but without any of the danger. I was always careful about addresses and stuff. There was no way the guys could actually track me down. And surprisingly, most of them were actually pretty nice. Just normal dudes who happened to have a thing for sniffing panties. That said, I still didn't want any of them getting my home address."

"Maybe that's what's going on in that other warehouse," I mused. "Maybe someone's getting a bunch of women together and working as a team to get it all done."

Read Between the Lies

"There's obviously a market for it," Ophelia said.

"You have no idea. I made my first sale in forty minutes when I started."

"I can't believe you all just stole a Kandinsky and all you can talk about is selling dirty panties on the internet," Sameen said, shaking her head. "Is Jean-Paul coming to get it?"

"I'm just going to text him now," Ophelia said, picking up her phone.

"What's the strangest request you ever got?" I asked Taylor. "I love art, but frankly, this is a more interesting story."

"Well, by the time I hit my third year, I had a method down, and I decided to focus on holidays. Christmas, Halloween, you know. For a while I wore a thong with little bells around the hem, which sold wonderfully, but I sounded like fucking Rudolph when I walked down the street."

This time it was Sameen's turn to spit out her coffee. She covered her mouth. "Sorry. But no. That can't be a real story. You're making that up."

"I'm definitely not. Halloween wasn't the best for sales, but Easter did wonderfully for me."

"Celebrate the birth of Jesus with cute bunny underwear," I said with a grin.

"They had a tail. I won't tell you what some of the men asked me to do to it."

"And that's my favorite holiday ruined. Thank you for that," Fiona said.

"You're married, aren't you? I can suggest a good gift for your husband," Taylor said, wiggling her eyebrows salaciously at Fiona.

"I literally cannot begin to fathom the kind of reaction Daniel would have if I suggested it."

"All I know is this conversation better be over by the time our food gets here, because I am *so* not listening to you all talk about selling dirty underwear online while I'm eating," Sameen warned.

"It was just a college job. But as I said, it's in my past now. I will tell you this, though: the username I used was PantyPrincess69."

I let out a groan. "Seriously?"

"What can I say? I knew my target market. And so does that warehouse owner, obviously."

"Do you have a boyfriend, Taylor?" Fiona asked. "Or are you single?"

"Single as of right now. I'm only looking for two things in a man: eight figures, eight inches."

"Well, Fiona got at least half of that," I said with a grin.

"I did. No word on the other half from me." Fiona made a zipping motion with her mouth.

"Oh, come on," Taylor said. "I just told you all about the sex work I did in college. The least you can do is tell me if I should be jealous of the man you snagged on two counts, or just one."

"Not a chance."

"You don't really want a rich man, though, do you?" Sameen asked Taylor. "We've known each other a little bit now, and you strike me as more the type who wants to make her own life."

"It's not about the money. It's about the man behind it. I need someone who's as nuts as I am. Do you know how easy it is to find a pushover? Boring. I need a man with the same ambition and drive as I do. Who's not afraid to bury a few bodies if it gets him what he wants."

"That sounds really healthy," I said.

"It's all I'd be able to handle. But sadly, no one is inviting me to meet the latest sociopathic billionaire, so I remain single and ready to…"

"Tinkle?" I offered, and Taylor threw a napkin across the table at me as our server returned with our food.

"All right, conversation over. Pretend we're all normal and act accordingly, or I'm going to invoice you all for my time, and it won't be cheap," Sameen ordered.

"Like Taylor's G-strings," Fiona giggled.

"Strike two," Sameel warned. I laughed as I grabbed my knife and fork and began to dig in. I ordered the Hangover, which was basically scrambled eggs over chili over hashbrowns, topped with salsa. Oh, and there was some cheese in there somewhere too. Basically, it was the perfect middle-of-the-night diner meal.

"You're such a buzzkill," Taylor complained.

"Lawyers usually are," Sameen replied. "We have to be, because we have clients like you."

"It's a little ecosystem of its own," Ophelia said with a smile.

"If you were really that uptight, you wouldn't have been involved at all," Fiona said.

"There's a reason I stay at the office rather than get my hands dirty like the rest of you. I'm uncomfortable actually committing crimes, but I do believe that everybody deserves the best possible representation. I would rather not know about the crimes ahead of time, but with Ophelia, I make an exception."

"How long have you been working for her?" Fiona asked.

"About two years now."

"Right out of law school?"

"Not quite. A few years later. Ophelia helped me out with a problem, and I'll always be grateful to her for that."

"I think that's how most of us got to know her," Fiona said wryly.

"Add me to that list," I said with a smile. "It's thanks to Ophelia that I'm not in jail for Jason Bergman's murder right now."

"Really? Wasn't that just a couple of weeks ago?" Taylor asked.

"Yeah."

"Wow, I thought the two of you knew each other for much longer."

I shrugged. "I guess we just hit it off straight away. She's just one of those people."

"Here's to all being Ophelia's people," Sameen said, holding up her coffee. "I never thought I'd find myself in a twenty-four-hour diner in the middle of the night celebrating an art heist, but here we are."

"This is the kind of thing I live for," Taylor said with a grin.

"Really? Committing crimes?"

"Making sure people get their due. Ophelia told me what was up. A guy like Kyle Wellman doesn't deserve that painting, and I'm glad it's been taken from him. I just wish those drivers had been a little bit more competent. Given me a little bit of a challenge. Losing them was easy."

"I'm so curious about what your childhood was like," Fiona said, shaking her head.

"I have a fun story about that."

"Is it safe to listen to while I'm still eating?" Sameen asked.

"Of course. When I was eleven, my little brother, who was eight, was on the local soccer team. He loved it. He was out in the yard every day practicing until Mom yelled at him that he had to come back inside. She'd always let him stay out longer than normal, though. She's Brazilian, so soccer's in our blood. Anyway, that year, Tommy made the best team in town for his age group, and he was thrilled. Second game of the year, he scored two goals, and he was basically the team's hero. Then, after the game, I saw one of the other dads talking to him. I thought he was congratulating him, so I walked up to them, but he was yelling. He told Tommy he was a shit player, that he would never amount to anything, and that he was taking opportunities away from the other kids on the team, like his own son."

I gasped. "You're joking."

"I wish I was. Poor Tommy started crying immediately. He'd always been a kind-hearted kid, not at all the kind of boy who would take that well. He saw me and told me he was going to quit soccer. I told Mom, and she talked him off the ledge."

"What did you do to the dad?" I asked.

Taylor's mouth tightened. "It took me a few weeks, since I was eleven, but I tracked down his email address. I created a fake profile for him on Ashley Madison and sent it to his wife. Three months later, that dad stopped showing up to those soccer games."

My eyes widened. "Wow. You did not come to play."

"He messed with the wrong kid. Tommy just loved to play soccer. Besides, the guy couldn't have been a great dad if he was out there bullying eight-year-olds. Or a great person."

"That's a good point," Fiona said. "I feel bad for a lot of the children I see. Their parents either don't care, or care too much. It's not healthy. I understand wanting your kids to be successful, but there have to be limits. And bullying someone else's child is just straight-up wrong. Although I'm not

Read Between the Lies

sure I would have taken that same route, especially at eleven."

"No, you would have hacked his computer instead," Ophelia replied with a smile.

"Sure. I started doing that for fun. But I did it because it was a challenge, not because I wanted to get revenge on anyone."

"Really? You never took revenge on anybody in your life with your computer skills?" I asked.

"Oh, I have maybe once or twice but not until much later in life. As a kid, I was very much all about the challenge. I would hack into places, have a bit of a look around, and get out. I was lucky too. I don't think I realized the potential consequences of what I was doing until I was much older."

"Come on, tell us a fun story," Taylor teased.

"Absolutely not," Fiona said with a chuckle. "Ophelia knows a few of them, though."

"And I've promised to take them with me to the grave," Ophelia replied solemnly.

"Well, if this breakfast was designed to tell me not to get on any of your bad sides, mission accomplished," I said with a grin. "I'm officially terrified of every single one of you."

"Even me?" Sameen asked, smiling. "I certainly don't mean to be terrifying."

"Oh, I know exactly what a good lawyer can do. Absolutely."

I looked around at the other faces at the table as the other women laughed. I wasn't sure I'd say I was friends with any of them, other than Ophelia. But there was a certain camaraderie that came from having committed a major crime together, and I felt a connection with these women.

I was so glad to have been a part of this. We'd saved a painting and were going to get it back to its rightful owner. And ideally, in a few hours, Ophelia and I were going to confront a killer.

Chapter 21

AFTER FINISHING OUR MEAL, THE FIVE OF US SPLIT up. It wasn't quite standing in front of the fountains at the Bellagio in Las Vegas. Actually, it was better. I liked the ladies in Ophelia's... I wasn't sure what to call it. Employ? Group of friends? Ragtag collection of vagabonds?

Whatever we were, we gelled well together. But I was also too aware that in just a few hours, I was going to have to work, and the adrenaline high I was on would be quickly replaced with sleep deprivation. Not to mention, Ophelia and I had planned on drawing out the killer today too.

It was all too much to handle at three in the morning, so I got home and immediately collapsed onto my bed, just barely managing to set my alarm before I settled in for a full three hours of sleep.

In what felt like seconds, the alarm went off, and

I groaned as I grabbed my pillow and pressed it over my face.

Why couldn't grand theft be a middle-of-the-day kind of thing?

Eventually, I pulled myself up to a sitting position and forced myself to get out of bed. I trudged the three steps from my mattress to the kitchen, where I gratefully found two of the coffees Lily had given me last night. I grabbed one and drank half of it in a single long gulp, not caring so much about the nuance of the flavors as much as wanting to get that caffeine into me, pronto.

I hopped into the shower, blasting myself with cold water to wake myself up, then changed back into the work clothes I hadn't worn in a few weeks and got ready for my first shift at the new donut shop.

It wasn't STD anymore. It was now La Bonne Bouche. When I worked under Elana, I used to have intrusive thoughts that involved me throwing myself in front of passing cars to get out from having to do my shift. I had a sneaking suspicion I wouldn't be feeling that way with Jenny in charge.

Sure, in any customer-facing job, a large part of the work was interaction with the customers in question, and there wasn't much a good manager or owner could do about how that went. But they still had the ability to make a difference to the overall morale of a team. And the raise was certainly a step in the right direction there.

Read Between the Lies

Glancing at the clock, I quickly headed out the door. In the haze of sleep deprivation, last night almost felt like a dream, like something that didn't actually, really happen. That feeling was enhanced when I went outside and everything seemed remarkably normal. There was no SWAT team ready to bust down my door. No police cruisers with lights flashing and sirens wailing as they sped past to go to the crime scene. No Twitter posts about the theft, no whispers from people in the street gossiping about the latest big shock to hit the city.

I knew it wasn't a fever dream, but for me to walk down to La Bonne Bouche knowing that I had stolen a fifty-million-dollar painting just a few hours ago, and that nobody even knew it had happened yet, was wild.

Did Kyle Wellman know yet? He had to, surely. Those goons in the van that Taylor had evaded would have reported back to him, without question.

I wondered if Ophelia was expecting him.

I reached La Bonne Bouche and took a couple of seconds to admire the front of the store now that the newspaper covering the glass had been removed. It looked well and truly inviting from the outside, like a little slice of Paris in the middle of San Francisco. Jenny had done a fantastic job and on such a short timeline. She would definitely rock this new role in her life.

Stepping forward, I knocked on the door, and

about ten seconds later, Jenny emerged from the back and ran over to unlock it.

"Thanks for coming," she said, somewhat breathlessly. "Sorry. This morning has been a bit of a disaster. We had a power outage in the middle of the night, and it didn't come back on until twenty minutes ago. So I've got the oil heating and ready to fry the donuts, but I haven't even started on that. And we only just got to work on the custard. We're so behind. I'm worried we won't be able to open on time."

"It's fine if you don't," I said, placing a comforting hand on Jenny's arm. "Remember, this is literally day one of a new business. Think of it that way. You can open it whenever you need to, and that's your opening day. If it's an hour or two later than you planned, who cares? That's not going to be the thing that makes or breaks this whole business."

"Thanks for talking me off the ledge. You're right. I just wanted everything to go perfectly today, you know? What if this is a sign from the universe, telling me that this isn't right for me?"

"What if this is a challenge from the universe, checking to make sure it is?"

Jenny took a deep breath. "Okay. Yeah, you're right. This isn't the end of me. It's not a sign that I'm going to fail. Thanks for the pep talk. Come on in. Let's get this show on the road."

Read Between the Lies

"It sounds like we don't have another second to waste."

I immediately stepped inside, and Jenny handed me a brand-new apron she'd bought: pastel pink with the new business name embroidered across the front. Very cute.

"This is yours. Oliver is in the back, making donuts. Do you mind giving him a hand? Rosa should be here any minute, and it'll be the four of us here today."

"Great," I said with a smile. I headed to the back, where the fryer sizzled away. Oliver had his back to me as he worked.

"Morning," I called out to him, and Oliver turned to me with a grin.

"Poppy. Nice to see you back at work. How's it going?"

"Great. You?"

"Couldn't be better. A couple of weeks off work was nice, although my bank account was starting to cry every time I opened it. The raise will help."

"It sure will," I said as I walked to the back of the room. "We're on donut duty today. How can I help?"

"I need some glaze and custard, and fast. I figure with the filled donuts, we're going to be kind of screwed for a bit, but if we can get a whole bunch of glazed flavors out quickly, we should be able to open on time."

"Got it," I said, immediately heading to the walk-in fridge for ingredients.

"Jenny made a list of donuts she wants for today, but she told me it was fine to scrap it and just get as many done of whatever flavor is quickest for now," Oliver called after me.

Even though I'd been away for weeks, I fell back into the rhythm of making the donuts like it was second nature. The ganache-topped donuts would be easiest to make, since they only required two ingredients. I grabbed as much cream as I could from the fridge then headed to one of the stainless-steel tables, grabbed some chocolate, and began measuring out ingredients.

Before I knew it, I had three types of chocolate ganache ready—dark, milk, and white—and Oliver was sliding over trays of sizzling hot donuts fresh out of the oil for me to decorate.

I slid on a pair of gloves and set about dipping the top halves of the donuts in dark chocolate, making two dozen right away. Then, grabbing a large spoon, I drizzled white chocolate over the top then finished them off with golden crisp pearls. It was nice to be back.

I took a second to admire my handiwork, then I carried the tray of fresh donuts to the front of the store. Rosa, another employee who worked part-time, smiled at me.

"Hi, Poppy. Nice to see you again."

"Same to you. I've got the first donuts ready."

"Perfect. I think we're just about set up out here, so I'll let Jenny know that we can open up whenever."

"Cool. There's more on the way too. We're working double-time back there, so we should be up and running soon."

"Sounds good."

I headed back to the kitchen to find another two dozen donuts ready for glazing. I figured these would make a good set of simple old-fashioned.

Jenny popped her head in the back. "By the way, I got a Bluetooth speaker for back here. As long as you don't put it on too loud, feel free to listen to whatever you want. I figure that might make the work here less monotonous," she said, reaching behind her and tossing over a speaker. "We're about to open."

"Good luck, Jenny. I know it's going to go great."

"You've totally got this," Oliver added.

"Thanks," she replied, smiling, but I could tell from the taut muscles in her face that while Jenny was excited, she was also nervous.

She headed back to the retail side of the store while Oliver pulled out his phone. "What do you want to listen to?"

I shrugged. "I'm pretty easy. Whatever you want is fine. As long as it's not country."

Oliver laughed. "No risk of that here. Okay, cool."

A moment later, Blink-182 blasted from the speakers. I raised my eyebrows. "I don't know what I expected, but it definitely wasn't that."

"Music peaked between 1995 and 2005," Oliver explained. "There was never anything better before that and never anything better since."

"Fair enough," I said, chuckling, as I went back to glazing, humming along to the song. Elana had never let anyone have music back here; it was nice to be able to dance along a bit to background music as I worked.

While I was working at warp speed to get as many donuts on the shelf as possible, time absolutely flew by, and before I knew it, Jenny came out the back to ask Oliver and me who wanted to go for their break first.

"You go," I said to Oliver. "I've got a batch of custard about to be ready for filling, so it'll work out well."

"Cool," he said, taking off his apron. "Thanks."

"How's it going out there?" I asked Jenny as I filled a piping bag with French vanilla custard.

"It's a little bit slower than a regular day, but that's to be expected. Most people won't realize we've reopened, after all. We've gotten nothing but nice comments about the décor, though. And I'm also thinking about changing up who we use for coffee. The brew we've got now is decent, but I figure if we can get people to come in just for the coffee, if we get a reputation for making a great one, that might inspire them to splurge on the occasional donut too. The coffee was more of an afterthought for Elana, but I want it to be a primary product here. Besides, if you're going to eat a luxury donut, you're going to want a luxury coffee to go with it."

"Yeah, for sure. The owner of the coffee shop at the bottom of my building wants to get to know you. You should ask her for recommendations. She's been running her café since the eighties, along with her wife, and they know a ton. I told her yesterday you were moving in with me, and she said you could come by any time if you wanted advice, or just to talk to someone else who knew what was up."

"Really? That's so nice of her."

"Yeah, Lily and Laura Belle are great. You'll love them. I have the key for you in my bag; remind me to give it to you before I go this afternoon."

"I will. I'm not sure when I'll be able to move in permanently, but it'll be in the next few days. I'll try to drop some stuff off tonight."

"Great."

At that moment, my phone pinged, indicating I had a text. It was from Ophelia.

The trap has been set. I texted Oliver to let him know we no longer consider him a suspect in Ellie's murder. Now, we wait, like lions perched in the bush, stalking our prey. Be careful.

I will, I texted back, my heart pounding. The stab wound in my shoulder began to ache, as if trying to remind me what happened the last time I ended up in a showdown with a killer. But I had to do this. Ellie had taken a chance on me, and I wasn't about to let her murderer get away with it.

"So, uh, somewhat unrelated, but Ophelia and I are hunting down a killer right now, and they might be coming after me, so it's probably a good idea to stay away until tomorrow."

Jenny raised an eyebrow. "Again? You're really making a habit of this."

"Well, to be fair to me, I hadn't actually expected this one," I said, raising my sling slightly.

"As long as you stay safe. Hey, you shouldn't be piping those donuts. I didn't even think of that."

"It's fine. It's a bit slow, but I've been managing."

"No, it's not fine. You have one functional arm, and this is very much a two-arm thing. I'm sorry, Poppy. I should have realized and given you an easier role this morning."

"You don't have to apologize. I would have said something if it was really a problem."

"I just don't want my employees to think I don't care. I know what it was like before. I don't want that to be the status quo here going forward."

"Don't worry, Jenny. We all know you're ten thousand times the boss Elana was," Oliver said as he walked back into the kitchen. "Forgot my wallet. But we're all grateful for the changes you're making."

"What he just said," I confirmed. "You're all

good, Jenny. Don't worry. And I really have figured out how to fill the custard donuts."

"Okay. Thanks, guys."

"It's fine to be nervous," I told her. "It means you care, and that's so much better than the alternative."

"Right. I'm going to head back out the front again. You're good here?"

"Always. It's nice to be back."

"It is, isn't it?"

Jenny headed back to the front, and I continued filling donuts as Simple Plan played in the background. Life could be worse. I was making money again. I had a plan to draw in the killer. The Kandinsky would be back where it belonged before long. Everything was coming together. If I was lucky, it would be tonight.

Chapter 22

My first day working at La Bonne Bouche completely flew by, and before I knew it, Jenny came to the back to announce that we didn't need any more fresh batches of donuts. Oliver went to the front to serve customers, while Jenny said I could head home, which I was grateful for after last night. I was exhausted, and I wanted nothing more than to go home and collapse onto my bed, but I knew I couldn't do that just yet.

"Here's the key," I said, handing her the set that had formerly belonged to Juliette. "It'll be nice to have a roommate again, but we'll be in tight quarters."

"Don't worry. As long as you're not nagging me to find myself a boyfriend and my own place, it's an improvement on living with my mom," Jenny said with a laugh. "I'll see you either later tonight or tomorrow."

"Sounds good. And congratulations on today. It's a big moment, opening your own business for the first time."

Jenny swelled with pride. "I only hope I can do it justice. It's been a learning curve, and it still doesn't feel real, but there was nothing as incredible as seeing people coming into a store I designed and wanting to eat here. Then complimenting the donuts, which I can't really take credit for. You and Oliver made them all, and they were Elana's recipes."

"True, but you had the smarts to keep them. This store might have been decorated in a way that was kind of soulless, but the recipes were top-notch."

"Yes, absolutely. And I plan on coming up with some new ones. I saw a recipe for a crème brulée donut the other day that I think would be incredible and a lemon meringue one that has potential too. But I'm getting ahead of myself. I figure let's make sure everything is up and running smoothly first."

"And no more power outages," I said, crossing my fingers.

"Exactly."

"All right, I'll see you tomorrow." I grabbed my bag and headed out into the street. I breathed in the fresh air. One of the things I loved most about San Francisco was the weather. Coming from Seattle, I was used to a fall season in which the sun didn't make an appearance. Once it disappeared behind the clouds in September, that was it. You could basically say goodbye to it until April. But here in San Francisco, things were different. Sure, there were days the fog liked to linger, and you had the odd sprinkle. But there were also days like this, when even in early November, the temperature topped out in the low seventies. Warm enough to get by with just a sweater and no rain jacket needed.

I'd take that over the Pacific Northwest's weather any day of the week.

Walking down to Ophelia's office, I kept an eye out. After all, our trap had been set. The killer was going to come after me at some point today. I knew that. I still couldn't believe it was her, in a way. Stephanie had seemed so nice. So devoted to Oliver. And yet it was all an act. She was a murderer who had killed Ellie and tried to frame Oliver for her death.

I couldn't wait to prove it and bring her to justice. Ophelia had texted Oliver to let him know he was no longer a suspect, knowing that he would pass on the news to Stephanie. Presumably, the police probably hadn't even visited them, and she would decide to take things into her own hands.

Since she already knew where I lived, Ophelia and I suspected she would try to get me at home. We had decided on a plan. I would stay at the office until it got late, late enough that when I got home, she could attack me without too many witnesses.

Not that that had stopped her the first time.

Still, we wanted to be sure she would come after me. She would undoubtedly try to leave some evidence on my body—maybe a knife with Oliver's fingerprints. Something a little bit more obvious than the last time.

Ophelia had figured it out when I mentioned the vase Steph had said she replaced. The color was all wrong. The vase hadn't been brown; it was red. And then, it clicked. The first time we were there, Steph kept trying to draw our eyes to the MIT hoodie that had been sitting on the table. It had been a deep red, the MIT color. But to someone who was colorblind, it would be the same color as the dark green hoodie the killer had worn. Steph must have bought it, thinking its color was identical to the MIT hoodie's and that it would instantly draw us to her boyfriend.

But it didn't, since neither one of us was colorblind. I hadn't picked up on the difference, but Ophelia had. And once she learned Steph was colorblind, Ophelia put two and two together and realized Stephanie had killed Ellie while wearing a hoodie and pretending to be Oliver. She wouldn't have wanted to take his actual hoodie, since he might have noticed it was missing. So she bought her own. And she was the murderer.

We weren't entirely sure of why, although Ophelia had an idea. She thought Steph believed Ellie and Oliver were having an affair and decided to kill two birds with one stone. Or, more accurately,

Read Between the Lies

kill one bird and send the other bird to jail for doing it.

Now, we'd set our trap. We figured Stephanie would be more likely to come after me than Ophelia. After all, she obviously already knew where I lived. Had she really been there by accident, or had she looked me up? Either way, she thought I was approachable and probably wouldn't hesitate to come after me again.

We would be ready.

I reached Ophelia's building and headed up the elevator. As soon as the doors open, I heard yelling.

"Where is it?" a man shouted. "I know you've got it. My security guys told me about you. What did you do with it?"

I rushed down the hall to find Kyle Wellman in Ophelia's office. He was standing, shouting at her, while she leaned casually back in her chair.

"I'm afraid I don't know what you're talking about," she replied smoothly.

"The Kandinsky. I know it was you. Someone broke into my warehouse last night and took it. White van."

"I drive a black Audi."

"Yeah, and of course it's impossible that you would get another vehicle. I know it was you. I know you did this. You took my painting."

"For one thing, you told me it was a fake. In fact, you *insisted*. So why are you so upset about its disappearance, which I assure you I know nothing about?"

"Just because it was a fake doesn't mean I don't want it back. That was a painting for my lobby. It looked good for investors. It was still a piece of art."

"Then why not call the police?" Ophelia asked with a smile. "I'm sure they'll help you get it back."

Kyle Wellman growled low in his throat then leaned forward, resting his hands on Ophelia's desk. "All right, fine. We both know it was real. You broke your promise and sent Interpol after me, and when they couldn't find the painting, you did. I don't know how you did it, but I know it was you."

"I did no such thing," Ophelia said, leaning forward herself. "But let me ask you something, Kyle: did you just buy the painting at auction, knowing it was hot, or did you hire the crew that stole it? Either way, it doesn't matter. You knew what it was when you bought it. Don't play dumb with me. We both know you did. And then, you placed it in your lobby as a perverted show of strength and arrogance. But let me tell you something: that painting is the perfect example of your kind. You are a taker. You take from society. You take from people. You see an item that belongs to the public, and you think that it would look so much better in your private collection, where the general public can't get to look at it. And that's how you treat business, isn't it? You collect money. You pay the fancy accountants so that they manage to hide your money in overseas accounts so you don't have to pay taxes. Like with the painting, you take from the public, but you don't give anything back. And so what does it feel like to have something taken from you? You're obviously angry. Now imagine how the rest of us feel."

"I don't steal from people," Kyle snarled. "I make *investments*. But I don't expect someone like you to understand that."

"Investments," Ophelia scoffed. "Please. Your private equity firm buys up private property like it's candy then charges exorbitant rent to people who can't afford it while purposely driving up property prices in the neighborhoods to keep newer buyers out. You're literally acting like a modern-day fiefdom."

"That's capitalism."

"It's greed, plain and simple. Is it legal? Yes. Is it wrong? Also yes. And by the way, the tax evasion part *is* a crime. But I'm not here to judge you. I'm just here to tell you that whoever took that painting just gave you a dose of your own medicine."

"What's this stupid lecture for? Do you think I'm going to suddenly see the light, sell everything I own, and donate it all to sick kids or something? Because newsflash: I'm not. I'm good at what I do, and I'm going to keep doing it."

"Oh, I don't expect you to change anything. You're not that smart. The lesson, however, is much simpler than that: you're on my radar, Kyle Wellman. Today, you lost a painting. It happens. I mean, I suppose it happens. I wouldn't know. I pay for my Kandinsky works. But if you continue to antagonize me, next time you might not be so lucky. I don't like being bullied."

"And I don't like being stolen from."

"Funny that. There's a museum in Lisbon whose director probably feels the same way."

"Are you threatening me?"

"That's an interesting question coming from a man who entered here telling me he was going to kill me."

"I didn't hear you deny it."

"I didn't. I'm not threatening you. I'm warning you. I know who you are, I know what you've done, and if you don't accept that you lost your painting, then I will make you hurt in ways you don't even know exist. Not physically. I won't tie you to a chair and rip your fingernails out. I will make you hurt so much worse than that."

It felt like the temperature in the room had just dropped fifteen degrees. Even Kyle, who up until now had drawn himself to his full height, imposing and trying to intimidate, pulled away from the table, crouching slightly, as if he'd just been slapped.

"You can't think you're going to get away with this," he warned her. "You won't."

"I've had far more dangerous people than you say the same thing, and yet I'm still here," Ophelia said, looking bored. I had to give her credit; not many people would take a threat like that so casually. "Now get out of here and be glad the only thing you lost last night was your painting and not your freedom."

"You promised you wouldn't send Interpol after me."

"I did. I lied. But you knew that, or you wouldn't have hidden the painting immediately."

"If I ever find out how you figured out where it was…" Kyle trailed off, obviously having run out of steam. "You'll…"

Then, without another word, he turned and stormed out of the office, barely offering me a glance as he brushed past me, audibly stomping down the hallway toward the elevator.

When the elevator door closed, I raised my eyebrows at Ophelia. "Someone's not happy."

"You're the one who should have gone into the investigative world."

I laughed. "You're way cooler under pressure than I am. I wouldn't have handled that as well. Do you think he'll try to come after you or something?"

"No. Men like that rarely do. They like to yell and scream their displeasure, but when it comes down to it, they're the type who don't like to get their hands dirty. It's the way he makes money, too: he runs a private equity firm who does a lot of predatory stuff, but he's an arm's length away from it, so he doesn't have to see the family that he's run out of their home. That's not the kind of person who will come here and actually attack me. He'll just yell."

"Still, I'm assuming you're careful?"

"Oh, of course. I've had multiple attempts made on my life. Don't worry; there is more security in here than you could ever imagine."

"That actually does make me feel better," I said with a nervous chuckle.

"Anyway, of the two of us, I think you're the one in more imminent danger. You had no problems today?"

I shook my head. "No. I was at work all day and in the kitchen at the back. There was no way she would have come for me there. I think you're right; she's going to wait until I head home."

"Yes. I agree. I'll be honest: part of me is very glad you've arrived here this afternoon. I was worried she might try to get to you on the way."

"Me too. She should still be at work, though."

"Yes, although she was able to leave without anyone noticing her absence when she killed Ellie."

"You looked into her alibi?"

"I did. Her boss did say she was at work that morning but that her office was private, that she could have easily slipped out for a few hours without being noticed, and that he does not micromanage his employees' lives as long as they get their work done."

"So her alibi for the first murder is nonexistent."

"Precisely. It is not proof that she committed it, however."

"Yeah. That comes tonight. Well, at the very least, she'll ideally be arrested for my attempted murder. And I hope that when she knows she's cooked, she'll admit to killing Ellie too."

"I want to know if my suspicion as to why checks out," Ophelia murmured.

"You think she was jealous, right?"

"Yes. I believe Stephanie thought Ellie and Oliver were having an affair. After all, they did have a history. And Ellie was keeping her relationship with Anna a secret, so there was no way for Stephanie to have known about it. I believe Ellie decided to make them both pay. She was going to kill Ellie, frame Oliver for her death, and watch as he was sent to prison for life. Unfortunately for her, it didn't quite work out that way. She overestimated the skills of the police, and she messed up her purchase of a hoodie that was supposed to lead to Oliver, due to her color blindness. We are quite lucky, in fact. Do you know how rare color blindness is in women?"

I shook my head. "I know it's much more common in men."

"Right. One in eleven in men, one in two hundred in women."

"Wow. That's… actually, that's more than I would have expected. It's not a lot, but I think she's the only person I know of who's colorblind."

"That's because nearly half the population who is colorblind isn't aware of it. Many people only uncover the condition well into adulthood."

"Really? I had no idea."

"Considering how severe Stephanie's color blindness is, I suspect that she is aware of it, but there's still the possibility she isn't."

"Weird. Okay, I'm hanging out here until you're taking me home later, right? Do you have somewhere I can sleep for a bit? I'm dragging."

"The office Fiona uses has a couch at the back of the room. By all means, feel free to use that. I'll wake you up when it's time to go."

"Thanks," I said gratefully. Stifling a yawn, I left Ophelia's office and went to Fiona's. I didn't even bother closing the door behind me. I just walked straight over to the couch and collapsed onto it, kicking off my shoes and shoving a decorative pillow under my head. I was asleep within seconds.

Chapter 23

I WOKE UP A FEW HOURS LATER TO THE SOUND OF a man's voice.

"I'll have my team come up and get the painting in a few hours. You should not have done this, Ophelia."

"I'll admit, I felt a little bit bad that I gave him the opportunity to hide the painting."

"Now we cannot prosecute him for its possession."

"No. He remains free, for now. A man like him, though, so brazen in his display of a stolen painting, has undoubtedly committed other crimes. I wouldn't be surprised if he has a whole collection of art of questionable provenance somewhere. It will catch up to him eventually. It always does. Especially once I'm aware of it."

"All the same, I'm glad to have the painting. It will be returned to the museum from which it was stolen. I assume, as always, that you would rather your name be kept out of this?"

"Please, feel free to take *all* of the credit," Ophelia said firmly.

"Does Wellman know you took it?"

"Yes. I'm quite certain he tried to get me to admit it on tape this afternoon. But it didn't work. He is a lumbering oaf without two brain cells to rub together, and he really thought he could trick me into admitting to what I did on tape. Besides, what was he going to do with it if I did? Go to the police? No, he obviously didn't think it through at all, but that's not a surprise."

"You'll be careful, then? Men like him have killed over less."

"Always."

"Good. It is always a pleasure working with you, Ophelia."

"*Merci*, Jean-Paul. Oh, how a day can change things."

"I was upset the other day. You forgive me?"

"Always."

"It is good to see you again. Take care, Ophelia."

"And you."

A moment later I heard the whirr of the elevator's mechanics heading back down to the ground floor. I sat up and rubbed the sleep out of my eyes just as Ophelia came in.

"Ah, good, you're up. That was Jean-Paul, just

coming to see the painting and to organize its pickup and return to Portugal."

"How's he going to explain to his bosses that he got a painting and can't arrest the person it came from?"

"That's a him problem, not a me problem," Ophelia replied with a wink. "Anyway, I was just about to come and get you. It's nearly seven o'clock. Are you ready? Are you still up for this? You can always back out."

I shook my head. "Ellie took a chance on me. I need to get justice for her. Let's do this."

Ophelia gave me a curt nod, and I got up, taking a slow, deep breath. I knew this was the right thing to do, but it was still going to be difficult. I was literally throwing myself at a murderer.

The two of us headed down to Ophelia's car. "How was your first day at the new job?" she asked as we got in.

"Good. Really good, actually. Jenny is great. Things were a bit slower than normal, but that's to be expected. I think word will get around that she's reopened soon."

"I'm glad to hear it. Let's run through this one more time: I will drop you off in front of your apartment. You're going to pretend that you can't find your keys in your bag and pull out your phone. That should give Steph enough time to come after you. Meanwhile, I will turn down the street to make it seem as if I've driven off, but I'm going to park a block away and come back. I should see her coming and be able to stop the attack on you."

"And when I pull out my phone, I'm going to press Record immediately, so that we'll have footage of what happens."

"Good. All right, we're here. Are you ready?"

I inhaled sharply. "Sure am."

"I'm going to be just around the corner. Thirty seconds behind you, tops."

"Cool."

I stepped out of the car and tried to act normally. After all, if Steph was in the shadows right now waiting for me, I didn't want to scare her off. I waved a casual goodbye to Ophelia then headed for the front door of my building. I rifled through my bag, pretending not to find my keys, when suddenly I spotted movement out of the corner of my eye. I looked up just in time to see Stephanie coming at me with a knife.

Uh-oh. This was not going at all how Ophelia and I had planned. Stephanie had barely waited; Ophelia must have just gone around the corner a couple of seconds earlier.

Stephanie lunged at me, and I darted to the left, narrowly avoiding the blade, which plunged into the door frame. She let out a yell and yanked it out, while I grabbed my keys from inside my bag.

"You killed Ellie," I snarled at her. "You're the one who did it."

"She deserved it. Oliver was mine! All mine!"

Read Between the Lies

"She wasn't dating him," I said with my best deranged grin, trying to channel Taylor. "She was dating Anna Mayer. Ellie and Oliver weren't a couple, you idiot."

My pronouncement obviously surprised Stephanie. "What?"

The split second of surprise took her off her guard, and I seized the advantage. I leapt forward and kicked her in the stomach, making her fall to the ground, knife still in hand.

I immediately unlocked the front door of the building and ran inside. But before I had a chance to close the door behind me, Stephanie was back on her feet, and she propped it open.

I raced up the stairs toward the roof. I just needed to buy some more time. I knew Ophelia could break through that lock in seconds now, so I wasn't worried about her following us. And while I wasn't in the best shape ever, I did live on the third floor of a walk-up apartment. Nothing in the world made you better at taking stairs than going up and down them every single day. Stephanie, on the other hand, lived with Oliver, in a house. She wasn't as used to the stairs, and I quickly put some distance between us.

"Get back here," Stephanie called out after me. "You've got to die too. Just make it easy on yourself."

I ignored her and continued running. I reached the roof and ran out, bursting into the fresh air, the sound of my feet against the concrete replaced by the hustle and bustle of the city below. Cars along the main streets, sirens in the distance.

I had no idea what I was doing. I was really just trying to buy some time for Ophelia to arrive. She couldn't have been more than twenty or so seconds behind me. I hoped she realized Stephanie had followed me inside the apartment building.

"It's over, Poppy," Stephanie said. "Time to die. I promise, I'll make it quick."

"Do you really want to do this? After all, Oliver didn't cheat on you. Ellie was in a committed relationship. They were totally platonic."

"It doesn't matter anymore," Stephanie snapped. "What's done is done. Ellie is dead. I killed her, but I can't go to jail for it. You know, and you have to die too. Oliver will go down for this. This knife has his fingerprints on it; he used it to make dinner."

She showed me the blade and the latex gloves she wore over her hands. "They'll find your body, he'll be arrested, and they'll link him to Ellie's death too. If it makes you feel any better, I don't actually take any real pleasure in doing this. It's not like I have anything against you. It's just necessary."

"You're right. That makes me feel so much better," I said, rolling my eyes. "But it's fine, really. Because you're not going to kill me. It's over."

At that precise moment, the door to the roof access opened, and Ophelia stepped out.

Read Between the Lies

Steph turned, looking surprised again. Her gaze moved from one of us to the other.

"It's over, Stephanie," Ophelia told her. "The police have been called, I have my phone out, recording this. We know you killed Ellie, and now you're going to go to jail for it. Put the knife down and come with us peacefully."

Stephanie's eyes darted around, like a cornered animal. "No! No, I can't go to jail. I can't."

"It's going to be fine. Just put the knife down."

Steph clutched the knife harder, and I knew beneath the latex gloves she wore her knuckles were white. "I can't. I can't, I can't, I can't," she kept repeating.

"It's going to be okay," Ophelia said. "Just put it down. The police are coming, and it'll all be over soon."

"Yes. It will."

With that, Stephanie sprinted toward me. Ophelia ran after her, and I darted to the right to get away, but Stephanie didn't change course. A split second later, I realized she had no intention of attacking me. Stephanie was going to jump.

This building was four stories tall. I wasn't exactly an expert when it came to knowing what heights were lethal, but I was pretty sure if she went over, Stephanie would have a very low chance of survival. Instinctively, I reached out toward her. I managed to grab the hood of her hoodie just as she went over the ledge with a scream.

The force of her full weight threw me forward, and if it wasn't for the two-foot-high ledge, I would have gone over as well. As it was, I was thrown against the concrete, and it took everything I had to hang onto the hoodie. Stephanie wasn't going to die. She needed to face justice for what she'd done to Ellie.

"Hang onto her," Ophelia ordered. I closed my eyes and tried not to think about how much pain I was in. Stephanie's weight was pulling down on me; there was no way I'd be able to pull her back up onto the roof. I just wasn't that strong, especially not with one hand.

Below, Stephanie was shouting. "Let me go! Let me die!" She was obviously struggling away, probably trying to get free of the hoodie so she could plummet to the ground below.

"You need… to pay for… what you did… to Ellie…" I called out with difficulty. My eyes were squeezed shut. I didn't know how much longer I could hold on. My grip was failing. Thirty, maybe forty seconds had passed. I didn't think I was going to hit the one minute mark.

Then, I heard Ophelia's voice. "Let go!"

I released my grip, and Stephanie screamed as she plummeted to the ground. I immediately got up and peered over the edge, watching the last second or so of her fall before she landed directly in the center of a dumpster, obviously pushed into place by Ophelia.

For a second or so I held my breath, wondering if that had been enough. The sound of garbage bags crinkling gave me the answer: Stephanie was alive.

I collapsed against the ledge of the roof. It was over. It was all over.

Epilogue

AFTER TAKING A MOMENT TO COMPOSE MYSELF, I rushed back down the stairs and into the side alley where Stephanie had fallen.

Ophelia was on the phone, obviously with the police. So she hadn't called them before after all. It was just a bluff.

Stephanie, for her part, had obviously given up on everything, and was now sobbing in the dumpster, encircled by garbage.

"You're getting pretty good at saving people's lives," Ophelia said with a smile when she hung up the phone.

"This one was kind of a team effort. I'm not sure she would have made it if you didn't get down that fire escape at warp speed and think to move the dumpster underneath her."

"I have the feeling she won't be especially grateful to us. But at least I don't believe she's going to try to hurt herself anymore. The police should be here soon. They'll take her into custody. That was closer than I thought it was going to be."

"Me too. She attacked me almost immediately. I'm glad you figured out where we were."

"There simply weren't that many places you could have gone. It didn't take me too long to get into your building."

"I figured you'd be pretty good at that. Still, I can't believe she threw herself off the building. She must have really felt stuck."

"That's the problem with revenge plays. If it doesn't work the first time, you get more desperate, and the more desperate you are, the more mistakes you make."

"In this case, the mistakes were a good thing."

"They certainly were. I think I hear the sirens now."

About a minute later, a couple of police cars pulled up outside the building, and two officers jumped out. Ophelia directed them toward Stephanie, and the two reluctantly dragged her out of the dumpster and arrested her. I couldn't really blame them for their reluctance; the odor was pungent.

"We're going to need a statement," one officer came and told Ophelia as the other dragged Stephanie to the waiting car. "You're saying she tried to kill one of you? And she was the one who murdered that lady the other day?"

"Yes," Ophelia replied. "We can tell you everything down at the station, tomorrow."

I looked past her to the cop car, where Stephanie was sitting in the back. Tears streamed down her face, illuminated by the red and blue flashing lights of the police cars. The sight would have been poignant if not for the piece of banana peel stuck in her hair.

I swallowed hard. It was all over. Stephanie had been arrested. Ellie was going to get justice. We had done it.

When I got back home, much later than I had hoped, I wanted nothing more than to collapse into my bed and go to sleep. After all, I had another big day tomorrow.

But first, I pulled open my laptop. I scrolled back to the beginning of my book document and added a dedication page.

To Ellie. Thank you for believing in me.

Book 3 - On the Slayed Page -

About the Author

Jasmine Webb is a thirty-something who lives in the mountains most of the year, dreaming of the beach. When she's not writing stories you can find her chasing her old dog around, hiking up moderately-sized hills, or playing Pokemon Go.

Sign up for Jasmine's newsletter now to be the first to find out about new releases, and to find out how Dot and Rosie from the Charlotte Gibson Mysteries met. http://www.authorjasminewebb.com/newsletter

You can also connect with her on other social media here:

Also by Jasmine Webb

Poppy Perkins Mysteries

Booked for Murder

Read Between the Lies

On the Slayed Page (coming April 2023)

Charlotte Gibson Mysteries

Aloha Alibi

Maui Murder

Beachside Bullet

Pina Colada Poison

Hibiscus Homicide

Kalikimaka Killer

Surfboard Stabbing (coming March 2023)

Made in the USA
Las Vegas, NV
01 August 2023

75509418R00177